THE BLACKSTONE CHRONICLES

PART 5
DAY OF RECKONING: THE STEREOSCOPE

John Saul

FAWCETT CREST • NEW YORK

A Fawcett Crest Book
Published by Ballantine Books
Copyright © 1997 by John Saul

Map by Christine Levis

All rights reserved under International and Pan-American Copyright Conventions. Published in the United States by Ballantine Books, a division of Random House, Inc., New York, and simultaneously in Canada by Random House of Canada Limited, Toronto.

http://www.randomhouse.com

Library of Congress Catalog Card Number: 97-90039

ISBN 0-449-22789-8

Manufactured in the United States of America

First Edition: June 1997

10 9 8 7 6 5 4 3 2 1

For Linda, with
emeralds and diamonds

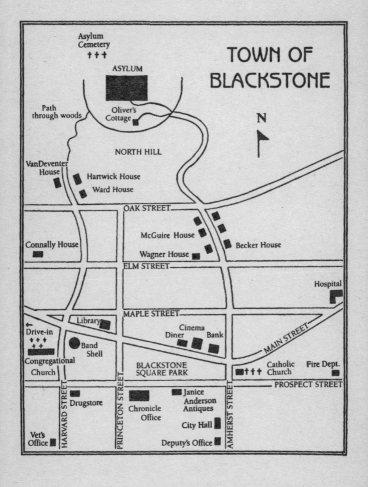

TOWN OF BLACKSTONE

Asylum
Cemetery
† † †

ASYLUM

Oliver's
Cottage

N

Path
through woods

NORTH HILL

VanDeventer
House

Hartwick House

Ward House

OAK STREET

McGuire House

Becker House

Connally House

Wagner House

ELM STREET

Hospital

MAPLE STREET

Drive-in
† † †
† †

Library

Cinema

Bank

Diner

MAIN STREET

Band
Shell

Congregational
Church

BLACKSTONE
SQUARE PARK

Catholic
Church

Fire Dept.

† † †

PROSPECT STREET

HARVARD STREET

Drugstore

PRINCETON STREET

Chronicle
Office

Janice
Anderson
Antiques

AMHERST STREET

City Hall

Vet's
Office

Deputy's Office

Prelude

*T*o any creature of the daylight, the dark shape would have been all but invisible as it moved through the inky corridors of the ancient stone building. Nor would any but the sharpest ears have heard it, so certain were its footsteps, so easily did it avoid any of the floorboards that might have betrayed its presence with the slightest creak.

Yet even in its silence and invisibility, the figure carried with it an aura of evil that spread before it like a chill wind, reaching into every room it neared, lingering even after the figure had passed by.

But unlike the dark figure's forays on earlier nights, when it had moved with eagerness through the halls and passages of its domain, on this night it crept almost reluctantly from its lair, drifting slowly through the corridors as if it had no wish to reach its destination. And indeed it did not, for tonight it would part with one of its most precious treasures, and though it was eager to revel in the madness the stereoscope would cause, still it was loath to give up the cherished memories the object held for it.

Prologue

Though he was barely eighteen, the boy had the heavy bones of a man who had long since reached his full maturity, and his large frame easily bore the muscles he had spent every day of the last four years building into indestructibility. Even now, though both his wrists and ankles were shackled to chains that were in turn affixed to heavy iron eyebolts mounted in the room's thick stone outer wall, he still exercised his body every day, maintaining his strength toward the time when he would escape from this room, slip free of the gray walls that surrounded him, and return to the world beyond.

The world where all his fantasies—all his darkest dreams—could once again be brought to life.

The room in which he was shackled held nothing more than the barest necessities:

A metal cot, as firmly fixed to the wall as the eyebolts that secured his chains.

A metal chair, screwed to the floor next to a metal table just large enough to hold the tray on which his food was brought.

A single barred window that pierced the wall, allowing him to gaze upon the village at the bottom of the hill with malevolent eyes.

A lone bulb, unshaded but protected by a thick glass and metal casing, was mounted in the exact center of the ceiling. The glaring light never dimmed, depriving him nightly of a haven of darkness in which to sleep.

A peephole in the door allowed the staff to keep watch on him. Though he could never see the eyes that observed him, he always knew when they were there.

He had been allowed only a single object to distract him from the endless empty hours his life had become: a stereoscope, brought to him by his grandmother.

"He's a good boy," the old woman had told his doctor. "He didn't do what they say. It's not possible. I'll never believe it." She had pleaded long and hard, and finally the doctor, convinced more by the size of the check she left behind than by her entreaties, agreed: the boy could have the instrument, along with the dozen images his grandmother had provided.

Since that day, the boy had whiled away most of his waking hours staring through the lenses of the stereoscope at the three-dimensional images. They were all pictures of home—the home they said he would never see again.

All the rooms were there for him to behold:

The big formal living room in which his parents entertained their friends.

The dining room, where two dozen people had often gathered for holiday feasts.

The nursery in which he'd spent the first two years of his life, before his brother had been born.

There were exterior views of the house too, of the enormous yard filled with spreading trees. Beneath these branches, he had first begun dreaming his wonderful fantasies.

His favorite image, though, was the one he was gazing upon today.

It was of his room.

Not this room, but his room at home, the room he'd grown up in, the room that had provided him refuge when the fantasies began.

The room in which he'd brought his darkest dreams to life.

It had been easy at first. No one noticed when the squirrels that had always annoyed him so much began to disappear from the trees outside his window; even the disappearance of a few yowling cats hadn't caused any trouble.

The next-door neighbors, though, and the people down the street had come looking for their dogs. Of course, he denied knowing anything. Why, after all, should he have told anyone that he'd skinned their pets alive, and hidden their bodies in the back of his closet?

When his best friend vanished, he had shed the proper tears—though he didn't really feel any emotion except relief that one more annoyance was removed from his life—and afterward decided not to bother with friends anymore.

For a while things had been all right. Soon, though, the little girl—his sister—started to annoy him, and he began to fantasize about sending her to join the others.

It made him furious when they finally came and took him away from his room. He struggled, but there were too many of them. Despite his screams and his shouted denials, they brought him up here and chained him to the wall.

They watched him.

He'd screamed every time they came near him, pouring out vivid threats of exactly what he'd do when he got loose and had his knives back. Finally, it seemed they decided to leave him alone. Except for the orderly who slid his meals through the slot in the door, he hadn't seen anyone for a long time.

Which was fine with him.

At least if they stayed away, he wouldn't have to kill them.

Not that he'd mind killing them, since killing what annoyed him had turned out to be the perfect way not only of satisfying his anger but of realizing his dreams.

He was still gazing at the image of his room at home, constructing a wonderful fantasy of what he might do if he were there right now, when he heard a noise at the door. Startled, he turned to see three men entering his room. He dropped the stereoscope and stood up, his fury at their invasion of his space already blazing from his eyes.

"Take it easy," one of the men said, glancing at the chains warily as if expecting the boy might free himself from his shackles. "We're only here to help you."

The boy's eyes narrowed, his jaw tightened, and he crouched low, ready to strike the moment they came within range of his fists. If he could just wrap one of his chains around one of their necks . . .

For interminable seconds no one in the room moved. Then, very slowly, the three men began edging closer.

Every muscle in his body tensed; his face contorted with fury.

"You can't win," one of the men said softly. "You might as well not even try." With a flick of his right hand that signaled his colleagues to act, he lunged for the boy.

Twenty minutes later, when the battle finally ended, the boy lay strapped to a gurney with thick bands of leather, his eyes still glittering with rage, his muscles knotting as he struggled against his bonds. Of the three men who had come for him, two had broken noses and the third a crushed hand. Although the patient had finally been controlled, he still had not been subdued.

"Do you understand what is going to happen to you?" the doctor asked. The boy glared up from the gurney and made no reply, except to spit in the doctor's face. The doctor impassively wiped the glob of phlegm away from his cheek, then began reading aloud from a document that had been issued by the court six weeks earlier. When

he finished his recitation, he glanced at the team around him. The three injured orderlies had been replaced by three others, and two nurses stood by. "Shall we proceed?"

The team in the operating room nodded their agreement. The orderlies moved the gurney into position next to an operating bench that had been constructed specifically for the procedure the doctor was about to carry out. A notch was cut in the bench, allowing the end of the gurney to slip under the open jaws of a large viselike clamp.

The boy's head was held immobile as the jaws were tightened on his temples.

Using a pair of electrodes, the doctor administered a quick series of shocks to the boy's head, and then, before the temporary anesthetic the shocks had provided could wear off, he went to work.

As a nurse peeled the boy's right eyelid back, the doctor found his tear duct and inserted the needlelike point of a long pick into it. With a sharp rap to the other end of the pick, he drove the point of the instrument through the orbital plate. Measuring the distance carefully, the doctor slid the pick into the soft tissue inside the boy's skull until its tip had sunk two full inches into his brain.

Satisfied that the tool was properly placed, the doctor expertly flicked it through a twenty-degree arc, tearing through the nerves of the frontal lobe.

The boy's body relaxed on the gurney, and his twisted grimace of rage softened into a gentle smile.

The doctor withdrew the pick from the boy's tear duct and nodded to one of the nurses. "That's it. His eye might be sore for a day or so, but frankly, I doubt that he'll even notice it." His work done, the doctor left the operating room.

One of the nurses swabbed the boy's eye with alcohol; the other taped a bandage over it.

While one of the orderlies released the clamps that held the boy's head immobile, the other two loosened the leather straps that bound him.

The boy did nothing more than smile up at them.

Three days later, when the bandage was removed from the boy's eye, he picked up the stereoscope and peered once more through its lenses.

The image of his room was still there, but it no longer looked the same, for when the doctor had plunged the pick into the boy's brain, it had cut through the optic nerve. He no longer saw in three dimensions, so the illusion provided by the stereoscope was gone. It didn't matter, though, for everything inside the boy's head had changed.

His fantasies were gone. Never again would he be able to make his dreams come true.

The dark figure lingered in the cold, silent room, his fingers stroking the smooth mahogany of the stereoscope's case. But he knew the moment had come. Reluctantly, with a last, loving caress to the satiny dark wood, he bent and placed the stereoscope in the fourth drawer of the oaken chest, sliding the drawer closed.

Soon—very soon—his gift would be in other hands. The hands carefully selected to receive it. Once more the past would return to haunt Blackstone.

Chapter 1

*E*d Becker shuddered as he gazed up at the grimy stone facade of the Asylum. "Sometimes I wonder if the whole idea of trying to turn this monstrosity into something nice makes any sense at all." Though it was an early Friday morning that promised a perfect spring day, even the bright sunlight couldn't wash away the ominous aura that seemed to him to hang over the building. "I have an awful feeling we might all wind up taking a bath on this deal."

Bill McGuire got out and slammed the door of his pickup truck. He barely glanced at the looming form of the building as he dropped the tailgate down and pulled the hand truck out of its bed. "You've been reading too many novels," he told Becker. "It's just an old building. By the time I'm done renovating it, you won't even recognize it."

"Maybe so." Becker sighed as they mounted the front steps. He and Bill, along with others, had returned here on Wednesday, and again yesterday, to search the cold, dark rooms and every inch of the ten-acre grounds for Rebecca Morrison, with no success. Now he said, "I'm starting to wonder if Edna Burnham's right and whatever's going on around here has something to do with this place."

As the contractor's face flushed with anger, the attorney wished he'd kept his thought to himself. It was too late now. "Look, Bill, I'm sorry," he said quickly. "I didn't mean to imply that what happened to Elizabeth was—well . . ." He floundered, struggling to find a way to extricate himself from his gaffe, but decided anything more he might add would only make matters worse. "I'm sorry," he said again. "I should have kept my mouth shut." For a second or two he braced himself, thinking McGuire might take a swing at him, but then saw the anger drain from the contractor's expression.

"Forget it," McGuire said. "I don't know why I still let it get to me. I mean, it's not as if I'm not hearing those ugly whispers from everyone else in town. It's not just Edna Burnham anymore."

It was true. In the two days since Germaine Wagner's body had been discovered crushed beneath the elevator in her own house, rumors had been sweeping through Blackstone like a virus, a contagion of fear and suspicion. Clara Wagner had been moved to a nursing home in Manchester only yesterday. Witness to her daughter's hideous death, she had suffered a massive stroke that robbed her of language; Clara would never reveal the events of that awful night her daughter had died. Germaine had been quietly buried as soon as the coroner had finished the examination of the body. By her own request, found neatly filed among Germaine's papers, there had been no funeral.

Steve Driver, the deputy sheriff, had searched every corner of Clara Wagner's house with as much energy as the fire chief had expended in sifting through the ruins of Martha Ward's place after it had been destroyed in a devastating conflagration a few weeks earlier. But his investigation proved equally fruitless.

There was obvious evidence of violence: nearly everything in Germaine Wagner's bedroom was overturned, her bathroom mirror shattered, blood everywhere. But even the criminalist Steve had immediately called in from Manchester had found no signs that anyone but Germaine had been involved. Blood samples from the bedroom and bathroom, from the stairs, from the Oriental carpet on the floor of the great entry hall were the same: all were Germaine Wagner's.

Most disturbing of all, Rebecca Morrison had disappeared. The only possible witness who might be able to describe these terrible events had vanished. Where was she—and was she in danger, if indeed she was still alive? Had Rebecca witnessed a dreadful accident—or a horrible crime? Had she fled in terror—or in guilt? Or had some unspeakable tragedy befallen her as well as the Wagner women? Searches of the town and the surrounding countryside had produced no trace of her, nor had appeals for information brought forth any clue. Even the Asylum had been combed, to no avail. Speculation burned like wildfire: Some said Rebecca had suffered a mental breakdown and turned on her benefactor. Others recalled that there was a dark side to Germaine Wagner's generosity, and that while it was true that she had employed Rebecca and given her a home when Rebecca's had burned down, she had also been treating Rebecca for years with the kind of patronizing attitude that no one but Rebecca would have tolerated for more than a minute.

Had Rebecca finally been pushed too far, into an act of cold-blooded murder from which she had fled?

Steve Driver found these whispered theories ridiculous. He'd known both Rebecca Morrison and Germaine Wagner for better than twenty years. He was unable to imagine Rebecca in the role of murderess. Moreover, she would never have been able to inflict the kind of wounds Germaine had sustained without injuring herself as well. The litter of broken glass in the bathroom alone gave the lie to that idea. Nor had he been able to find even a sliver of evidence that anyone except the three people who lived in the house were there that night.

Blackstone was pressing for answers, no one more so than Oliver Metcalf, and Driver had none, not a single thing that made any sense. On Thursday evening Oliver had burst yet again into the deputy's office, demanding a report of Driver's progress. At a loss, and before he could stop himself, Driver sardonically suggested that maybe Germaine had been the recipient of the same kind of "gift" that had brought tragedy into three other Blackstone houses over the last few months. To his utter shock, Oliver Metcalf's face paled.

"Oh my God," Oliver whispered. "It was *my* fault. I gave Rebecca a handkerchief. It had an R embroidered on it. . . . I—I thought it would be perfect for her."

"For Christ's sake, Oliver!" Driver said, astonished. "I was kidding! Don't tell me even you believe that crap Edna Burnham's been spreading around!"

Though both men would have been willing to swear they'd been alone in the deputy's office, the rumor of another "cursed" gift had swept like a plague through the town.

When the latest rumors had reached Bill McGuire, though, he'd dismissed them in disgust. Now he repeated to Ed Becker the same words he'd spoken to Velma Tuesday afternoon when he'd stopped in at the Red Hen for a piece of pecan pie and a cup of coffee after his tour of the Asylum with Ed and Melissa Holloway. "What happened to Elizabeth was a direct result of her miscarriage. It had nothing at all to do with the doll that showed up at our house. Megan still has the doll, and nothing's happened to her, has it?"

"Of course not," Ed Becker agreed. "And nothing's going to either."

Bill McGuire unlocked the Asylum's huge front door. As it swung open, Ed Becker felt a chill as a mass of cold air rushed from the building. Unbidden memories of stories he'd read as a boy blossomed in his mind, and he shivered as he remembered that a mass of cold air in a room invariably presaged a ghostly presence.

Or merely a lack of heat in a big old building on a

warm morning, he told himself as the chill passed as quickly as it had come. But when he stepped inside, it seized him again. The door closed, shutting the bright sunlight out, and the gloom closed around him like a suffocating shroud.

Suddenly he wondered if he really wanted the oak dresser they'd come to pick up.

"Getting to you?" Bill McGuire asked, grinning at the lawyer's obvious discomfort. "Maybe you'd like to wait outside while I go up and get the dresser."

"I'm fine," Ed Becker insisted, hearing too late the extra emphasis that belied his words. "All right, so I think it's a little creepy in here. So sue me."

McGuire laughed. "Spoken like a true lawyer." But then he too shivered, and found himself wishing he could just turn on the lights and wash the dark shadows from the rooms they were passing through.

Both men breathed a little easier as they came to the stairs to the second floor, if only because of the sunlight flooding through the windows behind the staircase. Yet even here they found a grim reminder of the building's last use, for the thick metal grill that had been placed over the windows decades earlier still cast forbidding prison-bar shadows on the bare wood floor.

It was as Ed Becker came to the top of the stairs that the hairs on the back of his neck stood on end and goose bumps rose on both his arms.

He knew, as surely as he knew his own name, that he and Bill McGuire were not alone.

An instant later, as McGuire too froze, he heard a sound.

It was faint, barely audible, but it was there.

"Did you hear that?" McGuire asked, his hand closing on Becker's forearm.

"I—I'm not sure," Ed Becker whispered, unwilling to admit how frightened he was. "Maybe . . ." His words died on his lips as he heard the sound again. This time there was no mistaking it.

Somewhere down the hall, in one of the long-abandoned rooms, someone—or some*thing*—was moving.

Ed Becker tried to swallow the lump of fear that blocked his throat.

The sound came a third time. It seemed to echo from one of the rooms on the left side of the wide corridor, halfway down the hall.

The room where the dresser is, Ed Becker thought, and his fear instantly notched a level higher.

Moving to the left so he was pressed protectively close to the wall, Bill McGuire began edging slowly down the corridor. Ed Becker followed hesitantly, his movement motivated less by bravery than by terror at the idea of remaining in the hall by himself.

As they drew closer to the room, they heard the sound yet again.

A scratching, as if something were trying to get through a door.

The door, which stood slightly ajar, suddenly moved.

Not much, but enough so that both of them saw it.

"Who is it?" McGuire called out. "Who's there?"

The scratching sound instantly stopped.

Seconds that seemed to Ed Becker like minutes crept by, and then Bill McGuire, closer to the door than Becker, motioned to the lawyer to stay where he was. Treading so lightly that he created no sound at all, McGuire inched closer to the door. He paused for a moment, then leaped toward the door and hurled it all the way open. There was a loud crash as the door smashed against the wall, then Bill McGuire jumped aside as a raccoon burst through the doorway, raced past Ed Becker, and disappeared up the stairs.

"Jesus." Ed Becker swore softly, utterly disgusted with himself for the terror he had felt only a moment ago. "Let's get the damn dresser and get out of here before we both have a heart attack." Retrieving the hand truck from the landing, he followed Bill McGuire into the room.

The chest of drawers was exactly where it had been on Tuesday afternoon, apparently untouched by anything more sinister than the raccoon.

Five minutes later, with the dresser strapped firmly to the hand truck, they reemerged into the bright morning sunlight to find Oliver Metcalf waiting by the truck. As they loaded it into the back of the pickup without bothering to unstrap it from the hand truck, Oliver eyed the old oak chest.

"You actually want that thing?" he asked as Ed Becker carefully shut the tailgate.

"Wait'll you see it after I'm done with it," Becker replied. "You'll wish you'd kept it yourself."

Oliver shook his head. "Not me," he said, his gaze shifting to the Asylum. "As far as I'm concerned, anything that comes out of there should go straight to the dump."

Ed Becker looked quizzically at him. "Come on, Oliver. It's only a piece of furniture."

Oliver Metcalf's brows arched doubtfully. "Maybe so," he agreed. "But I still wouldn't have it in my house." Then: "You guys want a cup of coffee?"

Becker shook his head. "I promised Bonnie I wouldn't be gone more than half an hour. Amy's home from school with sniffles and driving Bonnie crazy. How about a rain check?"

"Anytime," Oliver said.

Ed Becker and Bill McGuire got into the truck. As they drove away, Oliver caught one last glimpse of the oak dresser that stood in the truck's bed.

And as the image registered on his brain, a stab of pain slashed through his head.

* * *

The boy stares at the hypodermic needle that sits on the chest, not certain what is about to happen, but still terrified.

The man picks up the needle and comes toward the boy.

Though the boy cowers back, he knows there is no escape. He does his best not to cry out as the man plunges the needle into his arm.

Then blackness closes around him.

By the time the pain in his head had eased and Oliver was able to start back to his house, the truck had disappeared down Amherst Street, as completely as the image had disappeared from Oliver's memory.

Chapter 2

*R*ebecca Morrison had no idea where she was, no idea how long she'd been there.

Her last truly clear memory was of awakening from a nightmare to hear terrible noises coming from downstairs. She remembered leaving her little room in the attic, but after that her mind could provide her with only a jumble of images:

Germaine's room. A broken lamp on the floor. Bright red bloodstains.

More bloodstains on the stairs. On the carpet.

And an arm.

She clearly remembered an arm, sticking out from under the elevator.

Had Miss Clara been in the elevator?

She thought so, but even that wasn't clear.

She remembered running out into the night—she must have been trying to get help—but after that, everything was a blank.

The next thing she remembered was slowly waking up, not knowing whether she was awake or trapped in a dream of wakefulness.

She'd been cloaked in darkness, plunged into a blackness so deep it had seemed she was drowning in it, unable even to catch her breath. When her mind had cleared enough for her to realize she was not dreaming, was not dying, but was awakening instead in some strange, lightless place, her first terrified thought was that she'd been buried alive.

A wave of panic overwhelmed her. She tried to scream, but all that emerged was a muffled groan that jammed in her throat, causing her to cough and choke.

Taped!

Her mouth was taped, so she couldn't give vent to the coughing, and for a second it seemed as if her head might actually explode. Finally, though, she'd managed to control the coughing—she still wasn't sure how.

Slowly—very slowly—her panic had eased, only to give way to something even worse.

The tape wasn't just over her mouth—it bound her wrists and ankles as well.

She was on a floor—a hard floor, covered with no rugs or carpeting. In the total blackness, she could not judge how large or small the room she was in might be.

A silence as deep as the blackness surrounded her. As time crawled endlessly on, the eerie quiet became as frightening as the dark.

Then the cold began to wrap itself around her.

It was a cold she'd barely noticed when she first came awake. But as the minutes and hours slithered by, and she could neither hear nor see, the cold, her sole companion, edged closer and closer, engulfing her in its clammy arms, slowly invading not only her body but her spirit as well.

Soon it had seeped into her very bones so her whole body ached. No matter how she tried to writhe away from it, there was no escape.

Sleep became impossible, for whenever exhaustion and terror overcame her, and her mind finally retreated into unconsciousness for a moment or two, the nightmares that thrived on the cold chased after her, torturing her even in her sleep so that when once again she came awake, body and spirit woke even more debilitated than before.

Her sense of time deserted her; day and night had long since lost their meaning.

In the first hours—or perhaps even days—she'd thought she might starve to death. When she first awakened, she had been far too terrified even to think about food or water, but even fear must eventually give way to hunger. At some point the ache induced by the increasing cold had been punctuated by pangs of hunger, stabbings that eventually settled into a dull agony that attacked her mind as efficiently as it ravaged her body.

With the hunger had come thirst, a parching so powerful she thought she would die from it. How long would it take to die? How much longer before hunger, or thirst, or some unnamed evil that would strike from out of the darkness brought deliverance from this unending agony?

The hunger and thirst, and the terror of the darkness, the emptiness, and the nightmares would go on until she finally sank into an oblivion that, she knew, would be welcome once it came.

But until then . . .

A sob rose in her throat, but she quickly put it down, knowing it would only choke her once it rose high enough. And when she felt hot wetness flooding her eyes, she battled against it, refusing to waste so much as a single drop of water on something as useless as tears.

The very effort required to wrestle against her raging emotions somehow put her terror under control, and after an interminable period of time—Rebecca had no idea how long it might have been—she finally conquered the worst of the demons that had come to her out of the darkness.

Over and over again she told herself that she was still alive, and that soon—very soon—someone would come and rescue her.

But how long would *soon* be?

There was no way of knowing.

Again, she shook off a demon nightmare brought on by the cold and roused herself from the fitful sleep into which she'd fallen. But the moment she came awake, she knew that something had changed.

Something in the quality of the darkness was different, and she knew with utter certainty that she was no longer alone.

She lay perfectly still, holding every muscle in check, not daring even to breathe as she listened to the silence.

It too had changed.

No longer the empty, eerie silence she had awakened into before, now there seemed to be something—something not-quite-audible—lurking just beyond the range of her hearing.

And her skin was crawling, as if some primeval sixth sense detected watching eyes that her own could not see.

Her heart raced; her pulse throbbed in her ears.

Whatever lurked in the darkness drew closer.

An icy sheen of sweat oozed from Rebecca's pores, making her skin slick with fear.

And then she felt the touch.

A shriek rose in her throat as something so feather-light as almost not to be there at all brushed against her face, but once again the tape securing her mouth cut off her cry, and her howl of terror was strangled into a whimper.

The touch came again, and then, finally, the silence was broken.

"The beginning. This is only the beginning." The words were spoken with so little voice that they could have been no more than the whisper of a breeze, but in the silent darkness they echoed and resounded, filling Rebecca once more with indescribable terror.

The voice whispered again.

"Cry out if you want to. No one can hear you. No one would care if they could."

Then she felt the touch once more.

It was firmer this time, and it instantly brought back a terrible memory.

She had fled the house to get help. She was racing up Amherst Street, intent on getting to Oliver's house at the very top, just inside the gates to the old Asylum. And suddenly—with no warning—an arm had snaked around her neck and a hand had clamped over her mouth.

A hand, she had realized just before terror overcame her, that was covered in thin latex.

The same thin latex that covered the unseen finger now stroking her cheek.

The tape was ripped from her mouth.

Instinctively, Rebecca opened her mouth to scream, but before even the slightest sound came out, a voice inside her head gave her a warning:

He wants you to scream. He wants to hear your fear.

Exercising the control she had somehow gathered around her during the endless hours of cold and darkness, Rebecca remained utterly silent.

As she had for hours—perhaps days—she waited quietly in the dark.

The silence grew—stretched endlessly on. Though she could hear nothing, Rebecca could sense the growing fury of her tormentor.

She decided she would not give him whatever it was he wanted from her.

Not now.

Not ever.

Finally she spoke.

"You might as well kill me," she said, somehow managing to keep her voice from quavering even a little bit. "If that's what you're going to do, you might as well do it right now."

Again silence hung in the darkness like an almost palpable mass, but just as Rebecca thought she could stand it no more, the whisper drifted out of the void.

"You'll wish I had," it breathed. "Soon you'll wish I had."

She'd braced herself then, uncertain what to expect next.

All that happened was that the tape was put back on her mouth, and the hours of silence and darkness began again.

Now and then he came back.

He brought her water.

He brought her food.

He did not speak.

Neither did she.

Slowly, she explored the room in which she was being held, creeping across the floor like some kind of larva, snuffling in the corners with her nose, touching what she could with her fingers, though her wrists were still bound behind her back.

Every surface she touched was cold and smooth.

The room was totally empty.

She no longer knew how many times she had crept around its perimeter and crisscrossed its floor, searching for something—anything—that might tell her where she was.

There was nothing.

Then, a little while ago, the silence had finally been truly broken.

She heard footsteps, and the muffled sound of voices, and for the first time since she'd found herself in the silent blackness, she tried to cry out.

Tried, and failed, frustrated by the thick tape that covered her mouth.

A little later she heard the muffled sounds again, and once more she struggled against the tape, trying to rub it off against the floor, but finding nothing that would catch its edge long enough for her to rip it free.

Then the voices faded away, and the black silence once again closed around her.

Chapter 3

"Go all the way down by the garage," Ed Becker told Bill McGuire. "My back's already starting to hurt, and the closer we get to the basement stairs, the better."

Bill McGuire glanced over at the attorney. "Still got a coal bin? Maybe we could just slide it right on down. At least then it'll be in the right place when you decide to shove it in the furnace."

"Very funny," Becker groused. "But when I'm done, you won't even recognize it."

"Exactly my point," the contractor taunted. He slowed the pickup to a stop about ten feet from the Beckers' garage, and swung out of the cab just as the back door flew open and Ed's five-year-old daughter, Amy, came barreling out, closely followed by Riley, a six-month-old Labrador puppy that Amy had managed to convince her parents was "absolutely the only thing I want for Christmas. If I can just have a puppy, I promise I'll never ask for anything else again as long as I live so-help-me-God." While the campaign had worked sufficiently well so that the puppy had, indeed, taken up residence in the Becker house, Amy's father had yet to overcome the fear of dogs from which he'd suffered since he was his daughter's age. As the comparatively nonthreatening eight-week-old ball of fluff that Riley had been upon arrival developed into the immensely menacing—at least to Ed Becker—forty-pound medicine-ball-with-feet that Riley now was, Ed had become increasingly wary of his daughter's pet. Now, as Riley did his best to climb into Ed's arms and administer one of his specialty soggy face licks, the attorney who had never quailed before the most irate judge or angry client cowered away from the puppy's enthusiastic onslaught.

"Put him in the house, Amy," Ed ordered, reaching for authority although his guts seemed to have turned to Jell-O.

"He won't hurt you, Daddy," Amy replied with enough scorn to make her father blush. "He's just being friendly. He loves you!"

"Well, I don't love him," Ed muttered, now fending the dog off with both arms.

Riley, yapping happily and utterly unaware of the havoc he was wreaking on Ed's intestines, kept leaping at Ed's chest, enjoying the intricacies of this new game.

"Riley, *down!*" Bonnie Becker commanded as she thrust open the back door and joined the group around the pickup truck. The dog instantly dropped to the ground, though his entire body quivered with barely suppressed excitement as he gazed adoringly up at Ed. "Take him inside, Amy," Bonnie told her daughter. "Can't you see he's scaring your father half to death?"

Ed's embarrassed flush deepened as his daughter grasped the dog by the collar and began pulling him toward the house. Though the Lab, only a few inches shorter and no lighter than the little girl, could have dug in and refused to go, he happily submitted to his small mistress's tugging. Child and pet disappeared back into the house, and Ed, his courage fully restored now that the puppy was nowhere to be seen, attempted to recover a little of his dignity. "I am *not* afraid of him," he declared. "It's just that he's so big, he could hurt someone! He has to learn not to jump all over people!"

His wife nodded gravely. "You're absolutely right," Bonnie agreed. "Why don't you train him?"

Ed attempted a scathing look, failed miserably, then

flushed even redder when Bonnie giggled. "It's not funny!" he insisted, though now his own lips were starting to twitch. "He could really hurt someone!"

"Oh, he really could," Bill McGuire agreed, his expression deliberately deadpan. "I know I was scared out of my mind." He winked at Bonnie. "Did you see the nasty way his tail was wagging?"

"And the way his lips curled back when he tried to lick Ed's face," Bonnie added. "That was pretty scary."

"Oh, all right," Ed groused, finally recognizing he was going to get no sympathy. "So when it comes to dogs, I'm a wimp. So sue me." He went around to the tailgate of the truck, pulled it down, and began struggling with the big oak dresser. "You two going to help me with this, or would you rather just poke fun at me all day?"

"Poking fun sounds good to me," Bill McGuire said. "How about you, Bonnie?"

"I always think poking fun beats hauling junk furniture around," Bonnie agreed.

"It's not junk," Ed informed her. "It's solid oak, and it's at least a hundred years old, and—"

"And if it's not junk, then how come they gave it to you?" Bonnie asked.

"*Gave* it to him?" Bill McGuire asked, the question popping out of his mouth before he'd bothered to think of the implications of Bonnie's question. "Did he tell you we *gave* it—" Too late, he realized his mistake, then looked away so he could pretend he didn't see Ed glaring at him.

"How much?" Bonnie asked, suddenly far more interested in the dresser than she'd been even half a minute earlier. Moving closer to the pickup, she eyed the battered oak chest like a prizefighter sizing up an opponent, then offered her opening gambit. "I can't believe anybody would have the nerve to take money for this thing."

"You just don't know anything about antiques," Ed

parried, faking an offense as he tried to prepare his defense.

"Or Melissa Holloway," Bill McGuire added, though he wasn't certain whether his words would help or hinder his friend's cause.

Bonnie arched an eyebrow. "Melissa, huh? It's going to be even worse than I thought."

"That's hardly fair," Ed began, hoping to edge his wife into an entirely different arena. "In fact, it has all the earmarks of a very sexist remark."

Bonnie rolled her eyes. "It means I know Melissa, and frankly, if I had to place a bet on you or Melissa as a negotiator, I'm afraid I'd pick her. I love you very much, Ed, but I have a horrible feeling you paid a lot more than you should have for that dresser."

Seeing the slimmest chance at escape, Ed darted toward the opening Bonnie had given him. "What do you think I should have paid?"

Bonnie eyed her husband, then the dresser, then her husband once more, calculating how much he might have paid. A hundred? Maybe two? Surely not any more. She decided to let him off the hook. "Four hundred," she ventured, ready to repair his male ego by praising his shrewd bargaining when he proudly told her how much less he'd shelled out. When she saw him wince, she knew she'd guessed wrong.

"All right." She sighed. "The truth."

"A thousand," Ed told her, unable to look her in the eye.

Bonnie flinched, but then remembered the terror in Ed's eyes when they'd gone to pick up the puppy his daughter had wanted so badly. Moving closer to the truck, she pulled open one of the dresser's drawers and touched the dovetail joinery. "You might actually have made a good deal," she conceded. "When you get it restored, I'll bet you can sell it for twice that."

For the first time since he'd gotten out of the truck, Ed

Becker relaxed. "See?" he told Bill McGuire. "Even Bonnie can see how good a piece it is."

Ten minutes later, after Bill McGuire had unstrapped the dresser from the hand truck, helped Ed maneuver the heavy piece into his basement workshop, and headed back up the street to his own house, Ed began pulling the drawers out of the dresser, examining each one and assessing just how much work it was really going to take to bring the carved chest back to the beauty it had been a hundred years earlier.

It was in the fourth drawer that he discovered the mahogany box. Taking it out, he set it on top of the chest, then opened it as his wife entered the workshop. "My God." He whistled softly. "When was the last time you saw one of these?" Lifting the stereoscope out of the box, he held it carefully in both hands, turning it over so he could examine it from every angle. "It's perfect," he said. "Look—there's not a scratch on it."

Taking the instrument from Ed's hands, Bonnie held it up to her eyes and peered through the lenses, though there was no image to see. She tried working the focusing knob and the rack that would hold the cards, which moved easily along its track. And just as Ed had said, neither the brass fittings nor the leather and mahogany of which the stereoscope had been constructed bore any damage at all. With a little polish, the brass would gleam like new, and saddle soap would bring the leather back in just a few treatments. "Are there any pictures?" she asked.

"About a dozen," Ed replied. "Why don't you take it upstairs and show it to Amy? I'll be up as soon as I get the rest of the drawers out."

"Keep an eye out for treasure," Bonnie admonished him as she started for the basement stairs. "Who knows? Maybe some loony hid a fortune in there!" Easily ducking away from the mock swing Ed aimed at her, she picked up the mahogany box and took both it and the stereoscope upstairs.

Twenty minutes later, when Ed found Bonnie in the living room with Amy, both his wife and his daughter were absorbed in looking at the pictures. As he came into the room, Bonnie was handing the stereoscope to Amy. "What about this one?" he heard her ask.

Amy held the stereoscope up and peered through the lenses. "My room," she announced.

"Excuse me?" Ed asked. "What did she just say?"

"Her room," Bonnie told him. "It's what the picture's of."

Frowning, Ed crossed to the sofa where his wife and daughter were sitting. "What are you talking about?"

Bonnie looked at him. "It's the strangest thing," she said. "But all the pictures look like they're of this house."

Ed's frown deepened. "But that doesn't make any sense," he began. "Why would they be—"

"I didn't say it made sense," Bonnie told him. "In fact, I think—" She had been about to say she thought it was very, very weird, but remembered just in time that Amy never missed anything either of them said. "I think it's quite a coincidence," she finished, pointedly glancing at Amy, who was still peering through the stereoscope's lenses. "Let Daddy look," she said.

Reluctantly, Amy passed the stereoscope to her father, and Ed held it up to his eyes. All he saw was a large room furnished in Victorian style. "This doesn't look anything at all like Amy's room," he said.

"Not the way it is now," Bonnie agreed. "But take a look at this one." She lifted the card out of the stereoscope's rack, replacing it with another. "Look at the fireplace, and the bookcases, and the windows and door. Don't pay any attention to the furniture."

Ed gazed through the lenses at the three-dimensional image of a Victorian living room, filled with overstuffed furniture, tables covered with knickknacks, and ornate lamps with heavily fringed shades. But as he looked past the furniture at the features of the room itself, he began to realize that it appeared vaguely familiar. Then, slowly, it came into focus in his mind.

Take away the intricately patterned wallpaper, remove the thick velvet drapes, add paint to some of the wood-work, and completely refurnish it, and the room in the picture would be exactly like the one in which he was sitting.

Bonnie put another picture in the rack, and Ed Becker quickly recognized an earlier incarnation of his own dining room.

She changed the picture again, and he saw the back-yard, when the trees were smaller and the clapboards had been a darker shade than the pale gray they now were.

Finally he returned to the picture Amy had been looking at when he came in. Now he could see that it was, indeed, his daughter's room. His daughter's room as it might have been . . . when?

A hundred years ago?

Fifty?

He knew he had to find out.

Chapter 4

Steve Driver was seriously worried. His worries had been multiplying exponentially since Wednesday morning when Charlie Carruthers had arrived at the Wagners' to deliver their mail and discovered the door standing wide open and the house apparently deserted. It hadn't helped that instead of calling him immediately, old Charlie had followed his instincts and gone into the house, where he'd found Clara Wagner barely alive in her wheelchair and Germaine crushed under the elevator. In helping old Clara out of the elevator—a perfectly reasonable thing to do—he might well have destroyed evidence of an intruder. Evidence that could have stopped the clacking tongues that were, increasingly, suggesting that Rebecca Morrison was somehow to blame.

For all intents and purposes, the young woman had simply vanished off the face of the planet. God knows, he and Oliver, Bill McGuire, Ed Becker, and a party of other volunteers from Blackstone and even the surrounding towns had searched into the night on Wednesday and again all day yesterday before giving up.

Driver himself was absolutely certain that Germaine Wagner's hideous death had been a freak accident— though he still had no theory to explain why she'd been inside the elevator shaft in the first place—but he had no answers for those who were suggesting that Rebecca must have had something to do with it. After all, they asked, if she was innocent, why had she run away? Without doubt, some terrible scene had been enacted in Germaine's bedroom, but all the evidence indicated that whatever struggle occurred there, Germaine had been alone. The county coroner—a woman with a genius for excavating even the faintest evidence of a fight—had found nothing to implicate Rebecca Morrison, or anyone else.

Nothing had been scraped from beneath Germaine's fingernails; no telltale hairs or foreign fibers were found clinging to her clothes.

Which left Steve Driver, as well as everyone else in Blackstone, unable to account for Rebecca's disappearance. If she was abducted by someone who had killed Germaine, how had the killer managed to leave no trace of his presence behind?

And if she killed Germaine herself and then fled, why had she taken nothing with her? And left the door standing wide open, a sure signal to the first person who saw it that something was amiss inside the house?

Still, Rebecca was gone, he had no leads, and every hour the gossip was getting worse. Now, as he walked from his office to the bank, he wondered how best to conduct this interview. Would it be better to do it right out in front of everyone, where a few people might either overhear his questions or read his lips? Or should he conduct this part of his investigation in private, thus leaving everyone free to speculate about the questions he'd asked? He knew that technically the conversation should take place in private, but he also knew that there was one certain truth in places like Blackstone: people who talked behind closed doors had something to hide, and their conversations were therefore fair game for speculation.

Still, better to follow the rules, even if it did cause more talk.

"I wondered when you'd be in," Melissa Holloway said, rising from her chair as Ellen Golding showed him into the office Melissa now occupied in Jules Hartwick's place. "And I suspect I know what you want."

"Activity on Rebecca Morrison's accounts," Driver said as he lowered himself into the chair in front of Melissa's desk. He handed her a copy of the court order he'd gotten that morning instructing the bank to give him its cooperation.

"None, as of yesterday afternoon," Melissa told him.

"You already checked?"

Melissa nodded. "It struck me that if Rebecca were really trying to run away, she'd have to have some money. And she hasn't touched a dime."

"Nothing?" Driver asked. "Are you sure?"

"I'll check again." Melissa turned to her keyboard and typed rapidly. "But as of yesterday there hadn't been any withdrawals of cash, any checks, or any bank-card transactions." She fell silent for a moment as the screen in front of her came to life, then turned back to the deputy sheriff. "Still nothing."

Nor, Driver knew, could Rebecca have had much cash on hand, for even if she'd been in the habit of squirreling money away at home, whatever she might have hoarded would have gone up in the flames that consumed her aunt's house. In the few weeks she'd been living at the Wagners', there wouldn't have been time to build up any new reserves. "The truth of the matter is that I can't really imagine Rebecca running away from anything, anyway." Driver let out a sigh. "Knowing her, if she'd done anything to Germaine at all, she'd have called me herself."

"Then what happened?"

"If I knew, I wouldn't be here," Driver observed sourly. "It just doesn't make any damn sense. There isn't any evidence of a break-in, and even if an intruder had managed not to leave anything behind, I can't believe Rebecca wouldn't have screamed bloody murder."

"Or put up a fight," Melissa added as Steve, shaking

his head in a gesture of bewilderment and frustration, stood to end the interview. "Maybe it's the curse Edna Burnham keeps talking about," she went on, smiling as she rose to see him out of her office. Then, seeing the look on the deputy's face, she quickly apologized. "It was just a joke," she assured him. "But not a very funny one, huh?"

"No," Steve Driver agreed. "Not a very funny one at all."

The oak dresser was turning out to be a bigger project than Ed Becker had originally bargained for. A lot bigger. He'd come down to the basement right after dinner, expecting that within an hour or so he would have the dresser disassembled and all its hardware off. But after more than two hours, he was still wrestling with the top.

Of the eighteen screws that had secured the top to the dresser—a number Ed had initially regarded as a sign of "the kind of craftsmanship you just don't see anymore"— he had so far succeeded in removing only eleven. By now the "craftsmanship" Ed had admired only a couple of hours earlier had become "the kind of overkill only an idiot would indulge in!" Until Ed had begun swearing at the screws, Amy had been playing Daddy's helper, but then Bonnie summoned Amy upstairs, out of earshot of his four-letter imprecations. For the last half hour he'd been alone in the basement, with no one even to soothe his complaints. As he struggled with screw number twelve—whose recalcitrance was threatening to defeat him altogether—his mind was focused as closely on the work at hand as it had ever been on the most complicated of his legal cases, so when the door to the basement stairs opened, he didn't hear it.

Thus it came as a complete shock to him when Riley's

forty pounds of pure canine enthusiasm struck him a full broadside.

Three things happened nearly simultaneously:

His head reflexively jerked up, smashing hard against the frame of the dresser.

He sprawled out onto the basement floor, smashing his left knee hard on the concrete.

The point of the chisel he was clutching in his right hand sank deep into the flesh of his left palm.

Any one of the three would have been enough to make Ed yell; the combination of them all, piled onto the frustration he was already fighting, made him explode with fury. "AMY!" he bellowed. "Get this goddamn dog out of here! *Right now!*"

A second later his daughter came charging down the stairs. "Riley! Here, Riley! Come on, boy!" Wrapping her arms protectively around the big puppy, who was now happily licking his mistress's face, Amy glared at her father. "He wasn't trying to hurt you. He was only being friendly."

"I don't care what he was trying to do!" Ed snapped, getting to his feet and clamping the fingers of his right hand over the deep gouge the chisel had dug in his left palm. "Just get him out of here. If you can't control him, you can't keep him!" As Amy led the dog upstairs, her chin trembling as she struggled not to burst into tears, Ed moved to the laundry sink, wincing, to wash the blood from his left hand. He was rummaging around for something to wrap around his injured hand when Bonnie came down the stairs.

"For Heaven's sake, Ed, what happened down here? Amy's crying and says you threatened to take Riley away from her!"

"Well, if she can't control him—"

"She's not even six years old, Ed! And Riley's not even six *months*. Maybe you should learn to control your temper!"

Ed spun around. "And maybe—" But as he saw the anger in Bonnie's eyes dissolve into alarm at the sight of the blood oozing from his left hand, his own rage drained away. "It's okay," he quickly assured her. "The chisel gouged me, but it's not nearly as bad as it looks." Then, as Bonnie found a clean rag to wrap around his injured hand, he tried to apologize. "I'm really sorry," he said. "You're right. Riley wasn't trying to hurt me, and certainly none of it was Amy's fault. I—"

"Let's just get you upstairs and bandaged, all right?" Bonnie said. As they passed the dresser, she glared at it, already having decided that the damn thing was to blame for her husband's bleeding hand. "Incidentally," she said, "I think I know how the pictures got into the Asylum."

"Come on." Ed looked at her, surprised. "We just found them a few hours ago. How could you find out where they came from?"

"Edna Burnham, of course," Bonnie told him. "While you've been downstairs playing with your toys—"

"They're not toys," Ed interrupted. "They're tools—"

"Whatever," Bonnie said. "Anyway, while you've been playing with them, I've been on the phone. And according to Edna Burnham, you had a rather unsavory great-uncle."

In the back of Ed's mind, a dim memory stirred. "Paul," he said, more to himself than to Bonnie.

"You mean Mrs. Burnham's right?" Bonnie asked, astonished. "Who was he? And what did he do?"

"He was my grandfather's brother," Ed said. "And I'm not sure what he did. But I sort of remember Mom telling me about him once—how if anyone said anything to me at school, I shouldn't tell Grandpa. But nobody ever did, and I guess I forgot all about him."

"But why was he committed to the Asylum? What was he supposed to have done?" Bonnie pressed.

Ed shrugged. "Who knows? They could have locked

him up for anything, I suppose. Maybe he had a nervous breakdown."

"Or maybe he was a mass murderer," Bonnie suggested, her voice teasing. "After all, your fascination with criminal law had to come from somewhere."

They were in the bathroom now, and Ed winced as Bonnie peeled the rag away from his wound and began washing it with soap and water. "Don't you think if he'd killed someone, I would have heard about it?" But then an image of his grandparents came suddenly to mind: Stiff, emotionless people, the kind of New Englanders who never would have dreamed of airing any of the family's dirty laundry, even in private. If they'd had such a relative, neither one of them ever would have mentioned it. Indeed, they'd have probably stopped acknowledging his very existence on the day he'd gone into the Asylum.

The bizarre idea Bonnie had planted stayed with him for the rest of the evening. What if she was right? Not that Uncle Paul was likely to have been a mass murderer, of course, but what if he *had* actually killed someone? Maybe he'd heard more about his uncle than he now consciously remembered.

As he and Bonnie went to bed a few hours later, he was still searching his memory for any other scraps of information about his all-but-forgotten great-uncle, but whatever he might have been told had long since slipped away.

Every eye in the courtroom was on him, and Ed Becker resisted the urge to strut with pleasure at the discomfort he was causing the witness.

A cop was sitting in the witness box, just the kind of cop Ed hated most: a detective sergeant, the sort who assumed that anyone who'd been arrested must be guilty, and who therefore concentrated on searching only for evidence that would lend credence to his preconceived idea. Well, it wasn't going to work this time.

This time, the cop had gone after Ed's own great-uncle, and it was Ed's intention today to destroy not merely the detective's case but his credibility as well. By the time Ed was done with him, the detective would never be willing to get on a witness stand again, at least not in any courtroom where Ed Becker practiced.

And this courtroom was one of Ed Becker's favorites. Large and airy, it was in the corner of the building, and had four immense windows, all of which were open today to allow the sweet spring breeze to wash away the last of winter's mustiness.

But even in the cool breeze, the witness before Ed Becker was starting to sweat. Like a predator on the attack, Ed had caught the scent of the detective's fear.

Turning away from the witness for a moment, Ed gave his great-uncle Paul a confident smile, a smile designed to let Paul Becker know, along with everyone else in the courtroom, that for all intents and purposes the verdict was already won. When Ed was finished with this witness, the state would undoubtedly drop its case altogether. With another smile, this one accompanied by an almost fraternal wink to the jurors, Ed turned back to the witness.

"Isn't it true that you have absolutely no hard evidence that a crime was even committed?" he demanded.

The witness's expression turned truculent, his jaw setting angrily. "We found blood," he said. "A lot of blood."

"A lot?" Ed asked, his tone dripping with sarcasm. "What do you mean by a lot? A gallon? Half a gallon? A quart?" As the detective squirmed, Ed pressed harder. "How about a pint? Did you find a pint of blood?"

"Stains," the witness said. "We found stains on the defendant's knife, and on his bed, and on his rug."

Ed leaned forward, his face coming so close to the

detective's that the witness pulled back slightly. "So you didn't find a lot of blood," Ed said, his voice deadly quiet. "All you found were a few stains."

Suddenly, from a courtroom that Ed knew should be absolutely silent, tensed to hear what his next question would be, he sensed a stirring, followed by a ripple of laughter.

He spun around, searching for the source of the distraction.

And beheld his daughter's dog walking down the aisle from the door, carrying something in his mouth.

A second later Ed recognized the object that Riley was carrying. It was a leg.

A human leg.

On the foot, Ed could clearly see a white sock and a patent leather Mary Jane shoe.

The other end of the leg, cut off midway up the thigh, was still dripping with blood.

As Ed watched in horror, Riley pushed open the low gate that separated the spectators from the court, turned, and went to the defense table. Rearing up on his hind legs and wagging his tail, the dog dropped the bloody leg on the table in front of Paul Becker, then trotted from the courtroom.

Silence now. Deadly silence. Ed felt every eye in the room on him; they were waiting to see what he would do.

"It doesn't mean anything," he began, but before he could finish, another murmur ran through the room, and Ed turned toward the back of the courtroom, though he knew he was making a mistake even by looking.

"Guess maybe we just found some more blood, lawyer," he heard the witness say. Spinning around, he glared at the detective.

"It means nothing," Ed said, but his voice sounded shrill, even to himself. "The dog could have found—" But now he heard the courtroom door swinging open and he pivoted again, to see Riley coming down the aisle once more.

This time, carrying it as if he were bearing the crown at a coronation, the huge puppy held a head in his mouth.

A child's head.

A little girl's head.

The head of the little girl that Ed Becker's great-uncle Paul was accused of killing.

A great rage welled up in Ed Becker as he watched the Labrador puppy carry the head toward the table at which his uncle sat.

No!

He couldn't let it happen!

Not when he was this close!

Not when he'd had the jury in the palm of his hand and the prosecution's primary witness on the verge of admitting he had no real evidence at all.

His fury cresting, the lawyer charged toward the defense table and lifted the huge dog off his feet. With the animal still clutching the child's head in his mouth, Ed carried him to one of the open windows and hurled him out. He was already turning back to face the courtroom when he heard the blast of an air horn, followed by a howl of pain that chilled his very soul. Whirling back around, he leaned out the window and looked down.

All that was left of the dog was a shapeless mass of black fur, stained scarlet by the blood that was now oozing from his mouth.

A few feet away, the head the dog had been carrying lay on the pavement, staring straight up. But it was no longer the face of the little girl his uncle was accused of killing.

It was his daughter's face.

Amy's face.

A howl now rising in Ed's own throat, he turned away from the window, unable to look for even a second longer into his daughter's accusing eyes. But suddenly everything in the courtroom had changed.

He was no longer on the floor before the bench.

Now he was in the witness box, and everywhere he looked, his daughter was staring at him.

Amy sat at the prosecution table, gazing at him with condemning eyes.

Amy was on the bench, clad in black robes, already judging him.

Amy was everywhere, filling every seat, standing at every door, watching him from every direction.

She knew what he'd done.

She had seen it.

And now she was charging him, and prosecuting him, and judging him, and finding him guilty.

He rose up. "No!" he cried. "No!"

Suddenly, Ed Becker was wide awake, sitting straight up in bed, his body covered with a sheen of sweat. "No!" he said once more, but already the dream was releasing him from its grip. He felt exhausted, and flopped back on the bed, his heart pounding, his breathing ragged.

"Ed?" Bonnie said, sitting up and switching on the lamp next to her side of the bed. "Ed, what happened? Are you all right?"

He was silent for a long time, but finally nodded. "I—I think so. It was just a bad dream."

Bonnie propped herself up on one elbow. "Do you want to tell me about it?"

Ed hesitated, but already many of the details had slipped away from him and all he could really remember was the last moment, when everywhere he looked he'd seen Amy, staring at him, knowing what he'd done. "Go back to sleep, honey," he said, wrapping his arms around his wife. "It was only a dream. Something about a trial, and I think I did something to Riley. I can hardly even remember it."

Bonnie reached out and switched off the light, and

within a minute Ed felt her breathing fall back into the easy rhythm of sleep.

But he lay awake in the darkness for a long time. And even in the darkness, he could still see Amy's accusing eyes.

Chapter 5

*O*liver Metcalf was not sleeping well. Images were flickering all around him, as if he were in a carnival fun house gone dreadfully wrong: no matter where he turned, how he twisted, he could neither escape them nor see them clearly. But they frightened him nonetheless, for though they hovered around the edges of his vision, never coming into perfect focus, there was something familiar about all of them.

Painfully familiar.

He moaned with the effort just to *see*, the low guttural sound of a man exerting all the effort he can muster, to no avail. No matter how he tried, Oliver simply couldn't get a grasp on the images that floated maddeningly around him like smoke drifting in mirrors.

Finally, his frustration culminated in a spasmodic contraction of nearly every muscle in his body, and he came abruptly awake. Even before he opened his eyes, he knew something was terribly wrong.

Every bone in his body was aching with cold.

His eyes blinked open and for a split second he felt certain he was still caught in the nightmare, for around him he saw none of the familiar sights to which he usually awoke. Instead of the wall of his bedroom and the budding branches of the maple tree outside, he was staring at the silhouette of the Asylum, etched against a leaden sky. He was not in his house, but outside it.

Shaking off the last cobwebs of his uneasy sleep, Oliver slowly sat up, stretching first his arms and then his legs.

It was as he stood that he realized that not only did his limbs ache but his head did too. He braced himself against the great stab of agony that often followed the first telltale pang of one of his headaches, but the onslaught did not come. Instead, the dull ache in his head slowly ebbed away. He moved toward his house, but before going inside, felt an urge to look back just once at the Asylum. As his eyes scanned the dark building that loomed over his cottage—and his entire life—the strange images flickered once more through his mind.

But what did they mean? And why, since they were obviously embedded deep within his memory, could he not call them up as anything other than ghostly fragments of a past that seemed to be deliberately hiding from him? Turning away from the building at the top of the hill and closing the door firmly behind him, Oliver made his way to the kitchen and put on a pot of water for coffee.

As he waited for the water to boil, he glanced up at the clock: just after six A.M. Far too early to call Phil Margolis, even if the doctor would see him on a Saturday. But why call the doctor anyway? Whatever was causing his headaches was not a physical problem: the CAT scan had proved that.

No, it had to do with memories, and with the Asylum. And it had to do with his father.

As he poured the boiling water over the coffee grounds in his old-fashioned Silex, he remembered the case history he'd read a few days ago—a case history that had shown him just how little he'd really known about his father. Since then, he'd gone through most of the files he'd found in the attic, to discover they shared a sickening similarity. For years, patients in the Asylum had been subjected to the worst kinds of treatment, treatment that must have been utterly unbearable for them.

All of it done under his father's supervision.

Oliver absently poured himself a cup of coffee and took small sips of the hot brew as he thought.

Almost against his will, he found himself going to the window and once more looking up at the grimy stone building. What else had gone on inside it? What was hidden behind its walls that was so horrifying it prevented him from entering the building? Even as the question formed in his mind, he knew who would have the answer.

Draining the rest of his coffee in two big gulps—gulps that threatened to scald his throat—Oliver pulled a jacket off the hook next to the door to the garage and got into his car before he could change his mind.

Five minutes later he pulled up in front of the big house on Elm Street, just a little west of Harvard, in which his uncle had spent his entire life. Harvey Connally had been born in the master bedroom on the second floor of the Cape Cod–style house, and often announced that he had every intention of dying in the same room. "A man can travel the world all he wants," Harvey had been heard to say more than once, "but when he's ready to die, he shouldn't be far from where he was born." Though there were those in Blackstone who thought Harvey Connally's determination to die in the very bed in which he'd been born was a bit excessive, the old-fashioned sentiment was more typical of the town than not.

The house itself had become all but invisible from the street over the years, hidden behind a hedge that had been allowed to grow far beyond the basic demands of privacy. Whenever Oliver suggested that it be trimmed, though, his uncle shook his head. "After I die, you can do what you want with it. For now, I'll just leave it alone. I've got no reason to see what's going on outside it, and other people certainly have no need to look at me!"

Now Oliver opened the gate, then let himself into the

house with his own key, calling out to his uncle as soon as he was in the foyer.

"In the library," the old man's reedy voice called back. A moment later, as Oliver entered the book-lined room—his uncle's favorite in the house, and his own as well—Harvey Connally eyed him suspiciously. "A mite early for a social call, don't you think?" he asked. "I don't generally stir the martinis until the sun has set."

"I wasn't even sure you'd be up," Oliver admitted.

"I'm always up by five these days," Harvey replied. "An old man doesn't need as much sleep as a young one," he added pointedly. When Oliver made no reply, his uncle nodded to a silver tray that sat on a table in front of the wing-backed chair in which he was seated. "Help yourself," he said.

As Oliver poured himself a cup of steaming coffee, he felt his uncle watching him appraisingly, and as Oliver sat down, the old man issued his judgment. "You look tired, Oliver. Peaked. As if you're not sleeping well."

"I'm not," Oliver confessed. "And there's something I need to talk to you about." Though his uncle said nothing, Oliver was certain the old man's posture changed, that he became wary. "It's my father," he went on. "I want to know—"

"There's nothing you need to know about that man," his uncle snapped, his eyes flashing with anger. "After he died, I raised you to be a Connally, not a Metcalf! Do you understand? A Connally, like your mother! Like me! The less said about the man who was your father, the better." Harvey Connally's gaze fixed on Oliver with an intensity that warned the younger man he was treading on ground even more dangerous than he had expected, but he went on anyway.

"I need to talk about my father," he repeated. Choosing his words carefully, he told his uncle about the headaches he'd been having, and the strange half memories that seemed to accompany them.

"You should talk to Phil Margolis about this," the old man growled, his eyes hooding as he pressed deeper into his chair, almost as if he was seeking protection from his nephew.

"I did," Oliver said quietly. "And he hasn't been able to find anything wrong. But there *is* something wrong, Uncle Harvey. There are things I can't remember that I think I have to remember."

The old man snorted impatiently. "When you get to be my age, you'll know that some things are best *not* remembered." His eyes remained fixed on Oliver like those of an old wolf staring down a younger one. But Oliver didn't waver.

"I still need to know. I need to know what happened to my father. And I need to know what happened to my sister."

Harvey Connally studied his nephew for several long seconds, as if taking his measure. Finally, he seemed to come to a decision. "Your father killed himself," he said.

"I knew that," Oliver replied. "But I don't know why. Was it because he missed my mother so much?"

"I really have no idea," Harvey said, his tone betraying his reluctance to discuss the matter at all. "I suppose it could have been that. I also suppose"—and his voice hardened—"it could have been because the trustees had decided to close the Asylum."

Oliver felt his pulse quicken slightly. "I thought the decision to close the Asylum was made after my father died."

Harvey's head tipped slightly in assent. "There was no reason to tell you otherwise," he said.

"They fired him, didn't they?" Oliver asked. "The trustees found out what he'd been doing and fired him."

Again Harvey Connally's head tilted a fraction of an inch, but he said nothing more.

"And what about my sister?" Oliver said. "What happened to her?"

Harvey's attention shifted away from Oliver, as he pondered something.

"Did my father have something to do with my sister's death?" Oliver pressed.

Harvey Connally's gaze snapped back to Oliver. "I only know what he told me," he said.

"And what was that?" Oliver asked. "What did he tell you?"

Silence hung in the room for a long time. Finally, Harvey spoke, and though his words were uttered very quietly, they exploded in Oliver's head like blasts of dynamite. "It was your fault," his uncle told him. "It was just an accident, but it was your fault."

Oliver slumped in his chair, unable to speak.

Amy Becker's fists were firmly planted on her hips as she glared at her father with stormy eyes. "Why can't I go too?" she demanded.

"Because there isn't anything for you to do, and you'd just be bored," Ed assured her. "And I'll be gone only a couple of hours. When I get back, you and I can go for a hike. Maybe up in the woods behind the old Asylum. You'd like that, wouldn't you?"

"I want to go to the office with you," Amy insisted. "I want you to teach me how to be a lawyer!"

Ed reached down and lifted his daughter up so he could look directly into her eyes. "If you want to be a lawyer, you have to go to law school. And you can't do that until you've finished college. And you can't do that—"

"Until I finish high school, and I can't do that until I finish grade school." Making a face as she completed the familiar litany, Amy pretended to try to wriggle out of her father's arms. "I'll never get to be a lawyer!"

"Sure you will," Ed told her as he put her back down.

"Unless you decide to be something more fun, like a fireman or an astronaut. But all I'm going to do this morning is look at some papers. Okay?"

Amy sighed as if she were being asked to take the weight of the entire world onto her little shoulders, but then shrugged. "Okay. I'll play with Riley until you get back. But as soon as you come home, we're going for a hike in the woods. You promised!"

"I promised," Ed agreed, leaning over to kiss his daughter on the head. He straightened up as Amy skittered out the back door, then moved toward the kitchen sink, where Bonnie was rinsing the breakfast dishes. "And maybe when we get back from the hike . . ." he began, nuzzling the back of her neck as he slipped his arms around her waist.

"Ooh, promises, promises," Bonnie replied, letting her body shimmy against his. "Promise you won't stay more than a couple of hours?"

"Promise," Ed repeated. "I just have to review the final financing package for the Center so Melissa can give it to the feds. Should have done it yesterday," he added with a sheepish smile before Bonnie could remind him that he'd put in more time on the chest of drawers than his paperwork. Then, briskly: "In another week, maybe we can all start breathing a little easier around here."

Bonnie sighed. "I hope so, but sometimes I wonder if maybe we shouldn't just tear that horrible old place down and be done with it."

"Oh, Lord," Ed groaned. "Not you too! You're starting to sound like Edna Burnham!"

"I am not!" Bonnie protested. "Well, maybe a little bit. But I'm starting to think the whole idea of turning an insane asylum into a shopping center is a little creepy."

"It was Charles Connally's home before it was a mental hospital," Ed reminded her.

"I *still* think it's creepy," Bonnie insisted. Then she smiled. "On the other hand, if it'll help everyone in town earn a decent living for a change, then who cares what I think? *I* don't even care. Go get those papers done so we can all get on with our lives."

Giving Bonnie one more kiss, this time on the lips, Ed went out to the garage and got into the Buick.

Just as he always did, he started the car, glanced in the rearview mirror, and put the transmission into Reverse in a nearly seamless series of motions, then pressed lightly on the gas pedal.

The rear door had just cleared the garage when Ed felt a bump, followed instantly by a yelp of pain, then a scream of anguish. Instinctively slamming on the brakes, he jammed the transmission into Park and leaped out of the car, his first awful thought being that somehow he had hit his own daughter. A second later, though, as he saw Amy standing in the driveway and realized she was unhurt, he felt a wave of relief. His relief, however, was replaced with horror as he heard what Amy was shouting.

"You killed him! You killed Riley!"

Ed saw the black mass that was half-hidden under the car, and in an instant he was back in his dream, standing at the courthouse window, staring at the mangled body of Riley smashed on the pavement below, crushed beneath the wheels of a truck.

But this wasn't a dream.

And Amy, now on her knees beside her injured pet, was sobbing brokenly.

"No!" Ed gasped. "I didn't—" His words died on his lips as he saw a twitch of movement in Riley's hind leg.

Now Bonnie was next to him too, brought running from the kitchen by her daughter's anguished cries.

"Help me!" Ed told her. "He's not dead! If we can get him to the vet . . ." Leaving his sentence unfinished, he carefully drew the dog out from beneath the car. A faint whimper bubbled up from the animal's throat, but then, as if to apologize for the inconvenience he was causing, he tried to lick Ed's hand. "Oh, God, Riley," Ed said, his own voice now catching with a sob. "I'm sorry. I didn't mean to—"

"The car, Ed," Bonnie urged, gently guiding Ed to his feet. "Let's just put him in the car and get going." She pulled open the back door, and Ed laid the dog on the seat, ignoring the blood oozing from the corner of the Labrador's mouth onto the upholstery. "I'll get in back with him and hold his head," Bonnie said. "Get in front with your father, Amy. And fasten your seat belt!" Then she caught sight of her husband's ashen face. "Maybe I'd better drive," she suggested.

Ed shook his head. "I'll be all right."

Less than five minutes later he pulled into the graveled parking area in front of the building that served as Cassie Winslow's office as well as her home. From behind the house came the sound of half a dozen barking dogs and the cries of twice as many birds. Even before Ed was out of the car the veterinarian appeared on the porch.

"It's Riley, Dr. Winslow," Amy cried as she scrambled out of the passenger seat next to her father. "Daddy ran over him. Don't let him die! Please?"

Cassie Winslow dashed off her front porch and pulled open the rear door of the car. The dog's breathing was shallow, and his eyes had taken on a glazed look. "Let's get him inside," she said. "Ed, go ahead and open the doors for me. I'll bring Riley."

"He's heavy," Ed protested. "I can—"

"I have him," Cassie cut in, her voice firm but soothing. "Bonnie, why don't you see if you can't find a lollipop for Amy behind the counter in the waiting room?" Picking up the dog with an ease that should have been impossible for a young woman as slim as Cassie, she followed Ed through the waiting room and directed him to the examination room between the kennels and the laboratory. Laying the dog on the table, she expertly began running her fingers over him, feeling for broken bones.

"What happened?" she asked, glancing at Ed only for the briefest of moments before returning her concentration to the suffering animal.

As quickly as he could, Ed explained. "Is he going to be all right?" he asked when he'd told her all there was to tell.

Cassie Winslow arched her brows. "I'm not sure yet," she said. "I know one of his shoulders is broken, and at least three ribs. As for internal injuries, I can't—" She fell silent as Riley, with a rattling gasp, suddenly stopped quivering and lay still. Cassie felt for a pulse, looked into the Labrador's eyes, then gently closed them with her fingers. "I'm sorry," she said, her gaze finally shifting to Ed.

His hand shaking, Ed reached out to touch the big dog's body. "I'm sorry, boy," he whispered. "I'm so sorry." For a long moment he stood perfectly motionless, his hand still on the dog, as if his very touch might bring the animal back to life. But at last his hand dropped away, and he started back to the waiting room.

As he stepped through the doorway and saw his daughter looking at him, the memory of his dream exploded in his head, and as the voice from the dream cried out at him yet again, so also did his daughter's.

"You killed him!" Amy shrieked, instantly reading the truth on her father's face. "You killed Riley! You killed my dog!"

Ed went to his daughter, kneeling beside her, trying to comfort her, but she pushed him away and buried her face in her mother's breast.

"It was an accident, darling," Bonnie said softly, gently stroking her daughter's hair. "Your father didn't mean to do it. It was just an accident. He didn't mean to—" But as she looked up at Ed, the words died on her lips. Her husband's face had gone deathly white.

"I dreamed it, Bonnie," he said, nearly strangling on the words. "Last night, I dreamed I killed Riley."

"No—" Bonnie began, but Ed cut her off.

"I did," he said. "I dreamed it. And now it's come true."

Wordlessly, desperately trying to convince himself that there could be no connection between the dream and what had happened this morning, Ed knelt next to his wife and daughter and did his best to comfort the child whose pet he had killed.

But there was no comfort. No comfort for his daughter, and none for Ed Becker.

Chapter 6

A silence hung over the Becker house, but it wasn't the kind of comfortable silence that often settles over dwellings whose occupants are happy and content with each other. This was a tense silence, the kind of quiet in which people wait nervously, knowing something is going to happen, but not knowing what.

Bonnie had finally succeeded in putting Amy to bed, though the little girl had insisted that without her dog there was no possibility at all that she would go to sleep. She refused even to say good night to her father, to whom she hadn't spoken all day. Bonnie had sat with her for almost an hour, though, and finally Amy drifted into a fitful sleep.

When Bonnie came downstairs, she found Ed sprawled on the sofa in the living room, his feet propped up on the coffee table. Though his eyes were fixed on the television, she was sure he saw nothing of the flickering image on the screen. Sitting down beside him, she took his hand in hers and gave it a reassuring squeeze. "It wasn't your fault," she said quietly. "And I know it doesn't seem like it tonight, but Amy *will* get over it. And we'll get her another dog."

At first Bonnie wasn't sure if her husband had heard her, but finally he returned her squeeze. "I know." He sighed. "What's really freaking me is that I dreamed the whole thing last night before it happened."

Bonnie shook her head. "C'mon, Ed. It wasn't the

same as your dream. The circumstances were completely different."

For the first time since that morning, Ed managed a smile, though it was little more than a wry grimace. "Now you're starting to sound like me in a courtroom," he told her. "I always could split enough hairs to get the worst kind of sleazebags off hooks they should have been left dangling from."

"It was your job," Bonnie replied, though without an enormous amount of conviction. While she loved everything about her husband, even after having been married to him for nearly ten years, there were still some things she didn't understand, not the least of which was Ed's insistence that everyone, no matter how heinous his crimes might be, deserved the best defense that could be presented. *The prosecution will always twist things against the defendant.* He'd told her this so many times, the words were permanently etched in her memory. *It's my job to twist them the other way, so that in the end the jury has a shot at coming to a fair verdict.* The problem for Bonnie had always been that Ed was so good at twisting the facts, he often was able to get acquittals for people both of them knew were guilty. The final straw was a case that left such a bad taste in both their mouths that Ed had finally decided to give up his criminal practice in Boston and come back to Blackstone and a very quiet civil career. It was a capital case in which he'd won acquittal for a defendant accused of killing three children. Ed had convinced the jury that the police had somehow framed the man. The day after the acquittal, Ed's last criminal client had gone out and killed a fourth child.

"And I was good at my job," Ed said now. "Too good, as we both well know. But the plain fact is that last night I dreamed I killed Riley, and this morning I did it. You can't change the facts."

"Dreams don't involve facts," Bonnie insisted. "They

aren't anything more than your subconscious taking out the garbage after you've gone to bed."

"Even if you're right, it doesn't make me feel any better."

"Well, I'm not going to sit here and argue about it with you all night," Bonnie told him. "In fact, I think I'll go to bed. Want to come with me?"

Ed shook his head. "I'm going to stay up for a little while," he said. "Maybe I'll even go down and work on the dresser for a couple of hours."

Bonnie leaned over and kissed him. "Suit yourself. But whatever you do, don't keep on brooding. Things are going to be fine."

After Bonnie was gone, Ed reached for the remote control, intending to turn off the television set, when he saw the old stereoscope they'd found in the dresser, along with the collection of pictures, sitting on the coffee table. Ignoring the television, he picked up the stereoscope and pictures, then stretched out on his back on the sofa so the light of the table lamp would fall fully on the faded images printed on the cards. Dropping the first one into the rack, he twisted the knob until the scene came into focus.

It was the room that was Amy's now, though in the picture it looked little like the room in which his daughter was currently sleeping. Nor did it look anything like he remembered it from when he himself had been a boy and his grandparents had still lived in this house.

Yet there was something familiar about it, something that made him feel as if somewhere deep inside him, there was a memory of the room as it was in the picture, rather than as it was now. He studied the picture for several minutes, then put in another.

Again he had the sense that there was a memory lurking just beyond the fringes of his consciousness, but again he couldn't quite grasp it, couldn't quite pull it into a bright enough light to examine it.

One by one, Ed examined all the pictures, finally returning to a scene of the room he was in—the living room. It too held that vague feeling of déjà vu, though at least in that picture he was able to identify the source of the eerie feeling: two of the pieces of furniture—an ornate Victorian sofa and a large Queen Anne chair—had been in this room when he was a little boy.

Ed was still gazing at the picture when he slowly drifted into sleep.

He was back in the basement, working on the dresser.

Opening a drawer, he found a stereoscope, exactly like the one upstairs. There was a card in its rack, and Ed picked up the instrument and peered through its lenses.

This time he was staring not at a familiar room but at a scene in which a man was crouching over a woman almost as if he were about to make love to her. But there was a knife in the man's hand, and as Ed stared at it, its blade turned red. Then he saw that the woman's chest was oozing blood from at least a dozen wounds.

Suddenly, the man's face came into focus, and Ed recognized it as the face of a man he had defended a decade earlier.

A man who had stabbed his wife a dozen times, then left her—still conscious—to bleed to death.

Shuddering at the image, he dropped the stereoscope back into the drawer and slammed it shut, but when he pulled another drawer open, he found another stereoscope. This time he hesitated before picking up the instrument, but although he willed himself to resist, his hands seemed to close on it of their own volition. The image this time was of a fast-food restaurant. He felt a momentary sense of relief as he gazed at the scene of families seated at tables, munching on hamburgers and french fries. But then—like the image he'd gazed at before—it began to change, the happy faces on the children transformed into masks of terror, the black-and-white image horrifyingly reversed to its negative. A blinding flash, and then the floor was writhing with a tangle of bodies, and now crimson blood spouted from arms, legs, torsos. The blood of the innocent.

Ed had defended the man who had abruptly appeared in the doorway of that restaurant six years ago, carrying an automatic rifle with which he'd killed a dozen people in less than ten seconds, and maimed two dozen more. Within the privilege of their relationship, the man had calmly and with no remorse told Ed that he'd done it simply because "there were too damned many people in the place, and I was sick of seeing them." Not guilty by reason of insanity. His stomach knotting, Ed slammed the second drawer closed. He wanted to get up and walk away from the dresser, but it wasn't possible—something inside him compelled him to keep opening the drawers, keep pulling out the stereoscopes, keep viewing the atrocities his clients had committed.

The drawers seemed to go on forever, but finally he closed the last one. Having witnessed the final grisly scene, and looked once more upon the guilty face of another man he'd extracted from the jaws of justice, he at last was able to turn away from the dresser.

And found himself facing the same man he'd been defending in his dream the night before.

His great-uncle stared at him through the eyes of a madman; in his hands he cradled a double-barreled shotgun. Raising the gun, Paul Becker pointed it directly at him. "You got them off," he said. "You got every one of them off! Every one of them except me!"

As if in slow motion, Ed watched Paul Becker fire the gun. An explosive roar filled the basement, and suddenly there was blood everywhere. Ed could feel it, feel its hot stickiness as it oozed from the gaping wound the shotgun had torn in his belly, feel it running down his body to puddle at his feet. Somehow it had already flowed across the basement. It was smeared across the floor; it was flowing from the beams overhead. Every surface was dripping with it.

His blood. And the blood of every victim of every murderer he'd ever defended.

Now Great-uncle Paul was raising the gun a second time, aiming it at him, but this time Ed raised his hands, crying out. "No! I'm sorry! Oh, God, I'm sorry!"

It was the sound of his own voice that tore Ed Becker from the grasp of the nightmare. As he jerked upright on the sofa, the stereoscope tumbled to the floor.

He stared at it for a long moment, then reached down and picked it up. The card he'd placed in its rack before falling asleep was still there, and he started to raise the instrument to his eyes for one last look. But as the images he'd seen in the dream suddenly flooded back to him, blood-soaked and horrifying, he abruptly changed his mind.

Leaving the stereoscope on the coffee table, he went upstairs to bed.

But the dream still haunted him, and sleep refused to come.

Go to bed, Oliver Metcalf told himself. Just go to bed and forget about what Uncle Harvey said. But even as he silently repeated the words to himself for what must have been the twentieth time, he knew he wasn't going to be able to obey his own command. All day long he'd been trying to get his uncle's words out of his head, and all day long he'd failed.

Your fault . . . it was your fault.

But how could it have been his fault? He'd been only four years old. How could he have done something that killed his sister? "All your father ever said was that somehow the two of you had gotten hold of a knife of some kind." He paused, as if searching his memory. "You were playing with it. One of you must have tripped, and the blade . . ." Harvey Connally's voice had faded into silence for a moment, but then he'd made himself finish telling his nephew the little he knew. "The blade went into your sister's neck," he said. "Apparently you were so frightened, you ran away and hid the knife."

All day, Oliver had listened to his uncle's words replay in his mind, and slowly he began to understand what had happened to him. The gaps in his memory suddenly made sense—even now, so many years later, the mental image he conjured up of two small children playing with a dangerous instrument made him shudder, and when he tried to imagine the knife plunging into his sister's neck, the horror of the image was so great, he was unable to complete it even in his imagination.

What must it have been like when he'd been only four years old?

No wonder he'd blotted it out, hiding it from himself as thoroughly as he'd managed to hide the weapon from his father, and everyone else who'd searched for it.

No wonder people had looked at him so strangely all his life. Although his uncle insisted that Malcolm Metcalf never told anyone else what had happened, and Mallory's death had been officially deemed accidental, there would have been as many rumors about his sister as there now were about what had really taken place in the Wagners' house.

As had happened so often over the days since she'd disappeared, an image of Rebecca rose in Oliver's mind. Since her mysterious disappearance, he'd felt an emptiness inside him, a hole at his very core that grew larger with each passing day. His frustration had grown too, as he'd realized there was nothing—nothing at all—he could do to help her.

But of one thing he'd become absolutely certain: when

Rebecca was found—and he wouldn't let himself even think of the possibility that she might not be found—he would ask her to marry him.

But now, as his uncle's words echoed in his mind, he knew that when Rebecca returned, he couldn't ask her to marry him. Not until he'd banished the demons—the demons that brought the blinding headaches and the terrifying blank spots in his memory. This morning he had at last found the source of those demons.

And the reason he had not been able to make himself go to bed tonight was clear: he knew that the time had finally come to face the demons, and vanquish them.

Sometime during the day it had come to him, a slow and dawning realization of the reason he could not bring himself to enter the Asylum: the certainty that the "accident," the terrible thing that had happened to Mallory, must have taken place within those dark stone walls. From the moment he realized this, he knew that until he walked through those great oaken doors, he would not sleep. Yet as the afternoon had passed and daylight gave way to darkness, the courage of the sun had yielded to the shadowy terrors the moon brings with it. Now, as the clock downstairs struck midnight, Oliver knew he could put it off no longer.

He must enter the Asylum tonight or forever abandon hope of destroying the demons that haunted him.

Forever give up the hope of Rebecca.

Pulling on a jacket, he took his flashlight from its charger, checked to be sure the beam was at its brightest, then removed the key to the Asylum's door from the hook next to his own. Even then he hesitated, but finally pulled his front door open and gazed up at the shadowed building looming atop the hill, fifty yards away.

Dark, silent, it stood against the night sky like some great brooding monster, quiescent now, but ready to come to furious life the instant it sensed an unwelcome presence. Oliver started up the path, moving carefully, stepping lightly, as if the mere sound of his feet crunching on the gravel might be enough to bring forth whatever evil lurked within the blackened stone walls.

At the foot of the steps leading to the heavy double doors, he hesitated again. Already a headache was stalking the fringes of his consciousness. As he mounted the steps and inserted the key into the lock, the first waves of pain washed over him. Steeling himself, Oliver drove the pain back into the dark hole from which it had crept, pushed the heavy oak panel open, and stepped inside.

Turning on the flashlight, he played its beam over the shadowed interior.

Where? Where should he go?

But even as the questions formed in his mind, some long-buried memory seeping out from his subconscious guided him through the warren of offices until he stopped in front of a door.

It seemed no different from any of the others, yet behind this door, he knew, were the rooms that had been his father's office. His hand trembling, Oliver reached out, turned the knob, and pushed the door open.

Still outside the threshold, he let the flashlight's beam inch through the room, searching every corner it could reach for whatever dark menaces might be lurking in wait.

But the room was empty.

His heart pounding and his right temple dully throbbing, Oliver forced himself to step through the doorway, expectant, unconsciously holding his breath.

There was nothing.

No sound. No sense of an unseen presence.

Only three bare walls, long stripped of the pictures that had once adorned them, and a fourth wall, lined with empty bookshelves.

He had no real memory of this space at all, yet still felt

as though the room should be bigger than it was. But of course the last time he would have been in this room he had still been a little boy and it would have seemed huge.

Now it seemed small, and cramped, and dingy.

Crossing to a door that led to an adjoining room, Oliver paused, searching his memory for a clue as to what might lie beyond, but there was none. At last he grasped the knob and turned it, pulling the door open.

The flashlight revealed a bathroom.

A large tiled bathroom, still equipped with an old-fashioned, claw-footed bathtub, a toilet with a flushing tank pinned high on the wall—its pull chain long since disappeared—and a pedestal sink standing below an old-fashioned medicine cabinet with a mirrored door.

Oliver played the light into every corner of the room, but once again found nothing even slightly threatening. It was just as barren and grubby as the office next door. But then, as he was turning back toward the door, the beam of the flashlight struck the mirror above the sink. Through the layer of grime that had built up over the years, Oliver caught a quick glimpse of the bathtub.

Now, in the reflected glow of the beam, it was no longer empty.

Two figures, their eyes glimmering in the light, peered back at him.

Stunned, Oliver whirled around to bathe the figures in the flashlight's brilliant beam, but even as he turned, an explosion of pain erupted in his head. He staggered, reached for the sink as he fell to his knees, then slumped to the floor. The flashlight, released from his grip, clattered on the tiles and blinked out, and the room dropped into a blackness as dark as the unconsciousness into which the agonizing pain had driven Oliver Metcalf.

The Asylum was once again as still as death.

Chapter 7

*E*d Becker gazed dolefully at the glowing digits on the clock next to his bed. The last time he looked they had read 1:14 A.M. Now, unbelievably, they read 1:23 A.M. How could only nine minutes have passed in what had seemed to Ed like at least an hour? Yet the colon was flashing steadily, once a second, just as it always did.

Bonnie was sleeping peacefully beside him, not even making a movement or emitting a sound he could blame for his own sleeplessness, so he didn't have a decent excuse to wake her up. Finally giving up altogether on the idea of sleeping, he slid out of bed, pulled on his robe, and went downstairs. In the kitchen, he fished around in the refrigerator until he found a package of sliced ham, some turkey, and a loaf of bread. Five minutes later he carried his sandwich, along with a glass of milk, into the living room. Switching on the television set, he turned the volume down low enough so as not to disturb his wife and daughter, then restlessly switched it off again and picked up the latest issue of the *Blackstone Chronicle*, a special edition Oliver had hastily put out, most of it taken up with news of the death of Germaine Wagner and the disappearance of Rebecca Morrison. Though he'd elected to keep his own counsel, Ed privately agreed with those who suspected that Rebecca might have had more to do with Germaine's death than Steve Driver was currently thinking. It had been Ed's experience—and he would be the first to admit that his own experiences didn't make him the most objective of observers—that often it was exactly the kind of sweet, quiet woman, such as Rebecca appeared to be, who secretly harbored an anger that could explode into violence like the carnage that had swept through the Wagner house.

Oliver Metcalf, though, had carefully slanted the story to be so sympathetic toward Rebecca that she sounded like a saint.

Ed Becker didn't believe in saints.

On the other hand, it was exactly the kind of thinking he was indulging in right now—the assumption that not only did evil lurk within even the most innocent-appearing souls, but it would inevitably manifest itself in murder—that had finally led him to give up his practice and leave the darker side of Boston behind. So maybe Rebecca was every bit as innocent as Oliver presented her.

Putting the paper aside, he swallowed the last bite of his sandwich and, rising, carried the plate and glass back to the kitchen. He was about to switch off the light when he suddenly caught a whiff of something.

Gas!

Moving to the stove, he checked to make sure all the valves were tightly closed.

Every one of them was shut. The pilot light burned steadily blue.

Frowning, Ed glanced around the kitchen, then moved toward the door to the basement stairs. Instinctively reaching for the light switch as he opened the door, he reeled back as fumes surged out of the basement, nearly choking him. He slammed the door closed again, then broke out in a cold sweat as he realized what could have happened if he'd actually turned the light on. Any spark from the switch might cause the gas to explode. Then, as he remembered there was a freezer in the basement—a freezer that switched on and off automatically several times every day and night—his heart began to pound.

Out!

He had to get Bonnie and Amy out, right now!

Racing out of the kitchen, he bounded up the stairs, taking them two at a time. "Bonnie!" Shouting his wife's name again, he slammed open the door to their bedroom. "Get out!" he yelled. "Quick!"

Jerking awake, Bonnie sat up in bed. "Ed? What—"

"Don't talk! Don't ask questions. Just get out of the house! I'll get Amy!" As Bonnie finally started to get out of bed, Ed ran down the hall to his daughter's room, throwing its door open with enough violence that he heard the plaster behind it crack and fall to the floor as the knob struck it. Amy, already sitting up, was rubbing her eyes as Ed reached down and scooped her out of bed, snagging the blanket that had been covering her as well. "Come on, honey," he said. "I have to get you out of here."

Amy, still half asleep, tried to wriggle free. "No!" she wailed. "It's still night! I don't want to get up!"

Ignoring his daughter's words but tightening his grip on her, Ed dashed out of the room, coming to the head of the stairs just as Bonnie, now clad in a robe and slippers, was emerging from the master bedroom.

"What is it?" she demanded. "What's going on?"

"Gas!" Ed shouted as he started down the stairs. "The whole basement's full of it!"

A moment later he was fumbling with the chain on the front door, but Bonnie darted in front of him, her nimble fingers instantly freeing it from its catch. Then they were out of the house and hurrying across the front lawn. Only when they were on the sidewalk did Ed finally stop and lower Amy to the ground.

"Gas?" Bonnie repeated. "What are you talking about? How did you—"

"I couldn't sleep," Ed told her. "So I went down and

made myself a sandwich, and while I was cleaning up, I smelled it. I thought it was the stove, but—"

The blast cut off his words in midsentence, and he instinctively reached down and pulled Amy back into his arms as shards of glass exploded from the small light wells that served as the basement's two windows, and the long-unused access door to the coal bin blew off its hinges, allowing an enormous ball of fire to boil out of the cellar and roll across the driveway.

Shrieking, Amy wrapped her arms around her father, and buried her face in his shoulder.

"It's all right," Ed whispered into his daughter's ear. "It's going to be all right."

But in his head he was hearing the sound of the explosion over and over again.

It sounded exactly like the blast of the gun that Paul Becker had fired at him in his dream.

Rebecca wasn't sure what had awakened her; indeed, it was only the slow process of coming back to consciousness that told her she'd been asleep at all.

She wasn't afraid anymore—at least not in any way she'd been familiar with before being brought to the place that had become her dark, cold world. The things that had once frightened her—the unidentifiable sounds of the night, which only a few days ago would send goose bumps racing up her spine, or the imagined presences that might be lurking in the shadows on the evenings she walked home alone from the library—now seemed like old friends whose reappearance would bring her comfort in the total isolation into which she'd fallen.

Crazy, she thought. *I must be going crazy.*

She had lost all sense of time; had no feeling either of night and day, or of how long she'd been in the featureless room. In the muddle of her mind, there was no longer any difference between minutes and hours, hours and days, days and weeks.

Her wrists and ankles were still bound, but now she was blindfolded, and it felt as if her eyes were covered with the same kind of heavy duct tape that sealed her lips. She was certain she knew why the blindfold had been added: so her captor could see without being seen.

Now, as she came out of the restless sleep she'd fallen into minutes—or perhaps hours—ago, she tried to fathom what it was that had brought her awake.

A sound?

But there were no sounds; the tiny chamber that was her prison was as eerily silent as the palaces of death built for the pharaohs.

Yet she was filled with foreboding, sensing that if she held perfectly still, if she held her breath so that not even her lungs would disturb the quiet in the room, she would hear something.

She waited.

And then she heard it: The scraping of a key being fitted into a lock, followed by the click of a bolt being thrown. The door itself made no sound, but Rebecca, deprived of any visual stimulus, had grown sensitive to other things, and the slight change in the air currents as the door swung open felt like wind against her cheek.

And she could feel that she was no longer alone.

Still, she waited, and though she could hear nothing, she began to sense that whatever had entered the room was behind her now.

She felt a touch against her cheek, a touch so light she could almost imagine it wasn't there at all.

Then there was a quick movement, and she felt a slash of pain across her mouth. For a moment it was as if her skin were torn away, but then she realized it was only the duct tape that had been ripped off. A tiny moan escaped her lips. Instantly, a hand clamped over her mouth, silencing her.

The hand lingered, its pressure only slowly lightening, but Rebecca made no move, and finally it dropped away. A second after that she felt something touch her lips, and then realized she was being offered water.

Greedily, she sucked it up, swallowing every drop she was allowed.

A moment later the tape was once more pressed in place, but again the fingers lingered on her skin, and now Rebecca could feel the cold smoothness of the latex that covered them.

She held perfectly still, refusing to acknowledge the touch with any reaction. Finally, one of the fingers moved.

Involuntarily, Rebecca shuddered as the finger crept across her throat like the point of a knife. . . .

Ed Becker stared mutely at his house. Beside him, Bonnie was as silent as he, though their neighbors—who had appeared on the sidewalk before the first fire truck had arrived—seemed to all be talking at once. "What happened?" Ed heard someone say.

"An explosion," someone else replied.

"I saw a flash," a third voice said. "Helluva thing—lit up our whole bedroom. Scared Myra half to death!"

"Oh, it did not," a woman's outraged voice protested. "You were more scared than I was!"

"So if there was an explosion and a flash, where's the fire?" the first voice demanded.

And that was the eerie thing. There was simply no fire.

From the moment the gas had exploded in the basement, Ed had waited for his house to burst into flames, certain that by the time the first fire truck arrived, the building would have become an inferno like the one that destroyed Martha Ward's house only a few weeks ago. But as the sound of the sirens grew louder and louder, and not just one, but three fire trucks converged on Amherst Street, the house remained silent and dark, looking for all the world as if nothing had happened. As the fire trucks braked to a stop, their sirens were abruptly cut off, then three crews began pulling hoses from the reels on the trucks. Larry Schulze pulled up in the white Chevy Blazer that served as his chief's car and hurried over to Ed.

"What happened? Where'd it start?"

"It was gas," Ed explained. "I smelled it coming out of the basement, and got Bonnie and Amy out just before it blew. But I don't get it—how come the house isn't burning?"

"You mean 'how come it isn't burning *yet*,' " the fire chief corrected him. "Just because we don't see it doesn't mean it's not on fire." Dispatching one man to shut the gas off at the main, he beckoned to two others to follow him as he started down the driveway.

"I'm coming with you," Ed said.

The fire chief turned back, his stony expression clear even in the shadowy light of the street lamps. "No you're not," he declared in a voice that carried every bit as much authority as any judge Ed had ever dealt with in a court-room. "You're going to stay right here until I've gone around the house and then gone through it. When I'm satisfied there's no fire and that it's safe, then you can go in."

As Ed was considering the merits of trying to argue with the chief, Bonnie laid her hand on her husband's arm. "Let him do his job, Ed," she said. "Please?"

Ed nodded his thanks to Bonnie as Schulze and his men set off. In less than ten minutes they had circled the exterior and were back in front of the house. "So far it looks okay," the chief called as he mounted the steps to the front door, which was standing wide open. "Is the gas off?"

"Thirty seconds after you asked!" one of his men shouted back.

"Okay! We'll be out in a couple of minutes."

The crowd waited, finally falling silent as the fire chief inspected the house. When he emerged a few minutes later appearing just as calm as when he'd gone in, an audible murmur of relief rippled through the bystanders, except for two small boys who sounded sorely disappointed that they weren't going to see the firemen use their hoses.

"You got lucky," Schulze told Ed Becker as his men began rewinding their unused hoses onto the reels. "If you'd had the kind of trash in your basement most people do, you could have lost the whole house."

Bonnie Becker stared at the fire chief in disbelief. "You mean it's all right? It's not on fire?"

"That happens sometimes," Schulze explained. "You have to understand what goes on with gas. When it lights off, which probably happened when the freezer kicked on, it goes so fast that unless there's something in the immediate vicinity that's pretty flammable, it literally blows itself out. You lose all the windows, and the doors too, but that's about it. You can take a look now, if you want. But I'll go with you."

Ed gazed at the house, remembering just how close he'd come to dying that night. If the gas had exploded as he'd opened the basement door—

He cut the thought short, trying to shut out the image that rose in his mind of a boiling mass of fire erupting around him, snuffing his life out in an instant, or leaving him so badly burned he would have prayed to die rather than suffer the pain the flames would have inflicted.

Though he didn't want to think about what might have happened to him, he knew he had to go back into the house.

Into the basement, where the explosion had occurred.

With Larry Schulze following close behind him, Ed

started toward the front door. "Is it okay to switch on the lights?" he asked as they stepped into the foyer.

"Can't. I shut off the power, just in case. Use this."

Turning on the flashlight Schulze handed him, Ed moved cautiously through the foyer, shining the beam into every corner, barely able to believe the house had suffered no serious damage. But it seemed to be true— everything looked normal; nothing seemed even to have been disturbed. But as he entered the kitchen, he stopped short. "Jesus," he said, staring at the door to the basement.

Or, more accurately, what *had been* the door to the basement. It now was a heap of shattered lumber so torn by the explosion that it was barely recognizable as having been a door at all. All that remained within the frame were a couple of fragments of wood clinging to the hinges that had been half torn from the frame itself. "That's where I was standing not more than a minute before it blew," Ed said, his voice barely above a whisper as the unbidden vision of the exploding fireball rose in his mind once more. Stepping over the shredded wood that had been the door, he gazed down the stairs.

Oddly, the basement looked normal too. It wasn't until he'd started down the stairs that he realized he'd been expecting everything to be blackened. But apparently it had happened so fast that not even any charring had occurred.

As he came to the bottom of the stairs, he shined the light around and stopped short.

Blood!

There was blood everywhere!

His gorge rising, Ed braced himself against the wall as his knees threatened to buckle beneath him.

The blood was smeared on the walls, puddled on the floor, dripping from the beams overhead. But it was impossible! When the gas exploded, there had been no one down here!

Besides, the blood he'd seen before had existed only in a dream. Yet here it was.

First the explosion, sounding exactly like the shotgun Paul Becker had been aiming at him.

And now the blood.

The blood of the people his clients had murdered splashed through his basement as if in retribution for his having defended the undefendable.

But it was impossible! It hadn't happened! It was only a dream!

"Ed?" Larry Schulze was gripping his shoulder. "Ed, are you okay? I know the paint's a mess but—"

Paint?

Paint!

Or course! Not blood at all! Paint!

Though the fire chief was still talking, Ed Becker no longer heard his words. The strength finally coming back into his legs, he moved deeper into the basement.

As he looked around, using the flashlight to explore every corner, the same feeling of horror that had come over him when Riley died that morning crept up on him once again.

Though it hadn't been the roar of a shotgun, the explosion of the gas had sounded exactly like one.

And though the red stains on the walls and the floor and even the ceiling weren't blood, they looked no different from the terrifying crimson vision he'd witnessed in his dream.

It had happened again.

For the second time, his nightmare had come true.

Chapter 8

*T*he crowd in front of the Becker house dispersed almost as fast as it had gathered, and though Bonnie Becker knew the thought was uncharitable, she had a distinct feeling that at least a few of those who'd rushed out of their homes were just a bit disappointed that there had been so little to see. Within minutes after Ed and Larry Schulze emerged from the house, only Bill McGuire was left. Bonnie, feeling at sea, was perplexed—and perhaps just slightly resentful—that none of her neighbors had offered to take them in for the night. Was it possible they actually thought she would go back into the house tonight? Or take Amy back inside?

Bill McGuire read her expression perfectly. "You don't get invited to stay at anyone's house until you've been here for at least two generations," he explained, displaying the first semblance of a grin Bonnie had seen on his face since his wife died. "It's the price Ed has to pay for having married out of town. But don't worry—I married out of town too. You'll all stay with Megan and me. Besides, if I know Mrs. Goodrich, she'll have a pot of tea on."

Far too upset by fear and its aftermath to offer even the feeblest of polite protests, Bonnie gave Bill a hug instead. "I promise it won't be for more than a night or two," she assured him. "I just have to know it's safe."

Just as Bill had thought, the teakettle was whistling and Mrs. Goodrich was bustling about the kitchen as they entered his house, which was across the street. Amy, already having converted the night into a wonderful adventure, slid onto a chair at the kitchen table and demanded a glass of milk.

"Say please," Bonnie automatically instructed her daughter, but Mrs. Goodrich was already setting a tumbler in front of the little girl.

"Please," Amy parroted as her hand snaked out to take a cookie from the plate the old housekeeper offered.

Ten minutes later, with Amy making no more than a token protest against having to go to bed, Bonnie tucked her daughter in next to Megan McGuire. Megan was fast asleep, looking angelically peaceful with her arms wrapped around the doll that had been her inseparable companion since her mother died.

"It's so beautiful," Amy breathed, gazing at the doll's porcelain face. "Can I have a doll like that?"

"We'll see," Bonnie temporized. "I'm not sure we can find one. But maybe tomorrow Megan will share hers with you. Now, go right to sleep," Bonnie told her, bending over to kiss her daughter. "And don't wake Megan up. All right?"

"All right," Amy promised. But as soon as her mother was gone, she reached over to touch the beautiful doll.

"Don't," Megan said, her voice startling Amy, whose hand jerked back before she'd made even the slightest contact. Megan's eyes were wide open, and Amy realized she hadn't been sleeping after all.

"She's mine," Megan went on, "and she doesn't like anyone else to touch her. She doesn't like it one bit."

Megan's eyes closed and she said nothing else, but for a long time Amy lay awake. She stared at the doll. In the dim light from the street lamp outside, it almost seemed to be sleeping. But Megan's words kept echoing in her mind.

She didn't try to touch the doll again.

* * *

"It happened again."

Ed and Bonnie were in the McGuire guest room. Bonnie was already in bed, and Ed was standing at the window, gazing out at the house across the street and one lot down the slope. His house. His sanctuary, meant to provide shelter from the storms of daily life as much as from winter's icy blasts. In the last twenty-four hours his refuge had become instead a place where his nightmares came true.

"What happened?" Bonnie asked, though her heart was beating faster in anticipation of his reply.

"I dreamed it." Ed turned away from the window and sat on the edge of the bed. In the shadowy darkness of the room, he told her about the dream he'd had, and what he'd seen in the basement only a little while ago, when he and Larry Schulze had gone down to assess the damage.

"But it wasn't a gunshot," Bonnie insisted when Ed was finished. "And it wasn't blood. It was *paint,* Ed. It was just a can of paint whose lid got knocked off in the explosion."

"But—"

"But darling, it really *was* just a dream." Feeling utterly exhausted as the remembered terror of the explosion closed in on her, she said softly, "It will all seem different in the morning. Can't we talk about it then? Please?"

Ed hesitated, but as Bonnie held her arms out to him, he slipped into bed beside her, holding her close. She was right, he decided as he kissed her gently. In the bright light of day, none of it would seem so terrible. And, in truth, there had been no permanent damage, nothing they wouldn't easily recover from. Tomorrow they'd look for a new puppy for Amy, and with a couple hours' work the mess in the basement would disappear as completely as if the explosion had never happened. Bill McGuire had already promised to put in an automatic detection system to guard them against another accident. In a few days everything would be back to normal. As he felt Bonnie's breathing drift into the gentle rhythm of sleep, Ed Becker closed his eyes, yielding to oblivion.

Ed stood on the sidewalk, staring at the house.

Around him the night had become eerily quiet, as if the explosion had silenced every living thing in Blackstone.

Ed knew he should turn around and go back to Bill McGuire's house, slip back into bed with Bonnie, and let himself surrender to sleep. Instead, he moved toward the house, irresistibly drawn inside.

His house—yet not his house.

In the living room, all the furniture he and Bonnie had brought with them from Boston was gone, and the heavy Victorian decorations from the long-ago days when his grandmother had lived here were all back in place. The room looked exactly as it had when he'd viewed the picture in the stereoscope. The stereoscope itself sat on a mahogany gateleg table upon which a lace cloth had been spread. Moving closer to the table, Ed lifted the cloth and ran his fingers appreciatively over the perfect satin finish. There was a drawer at one end of the table, and Ed's hands closed on its pull. He hesitated, remembering the carnage let loose when, in his dream, he'd pulled open the drawers of the oak chest from the Asylum. Yet even as his mind cried out against temptation, Ed's trembling fingers slid the drawer open.

He found himself gazing at a .38 caliber pistol.

The pistol was clutched by a hand hacked off at the wrist, blood dripping from its severed veins.

Shuddering, he slammed the drawer shut. He stood still, waiting for the sick feeling in his stomach to pass.

It was not there, he told himself. I only imagined it.

But he didn't try to open the drawer again, instead dropping the tablecloth back in place to conceal the drawer, to make it disappear.

He left the living room and moved into the dining room. A gleaming cherry-wood table surrounded by eight armchairs stood where only a few hours before his own teak table had been. Against the wall a Victorian breakfront was filled with Limoges china in an ornate pattern of royal blue and gold. On one shelf three dozen heavy crystal goblets glittered in the dim light.

He reached for a glass. As he took it, it filled with blood.

Dropping it, Ed spun around. The table, bare only a moment ago, was set now as if for a feast. Twin candelabra, each of them glowing with a dozen candles, cast a warm glow over an elegant display of silver and crystal.

At each place, a serving plate had been set, and on each plate there was a single object.

The severed heads of eight of Ed Becker's clients stared at him with empty eyes. Their lips were stretched back from their teeth in grim parodies of smiles, and pools of blood filled the plates upon which they sat.

"No!" The word caught in his throat and emerged only as a strangled grunt. Backing out of the dining room, he turned to flee, but instead of taking him out of the house, his legs carried him up the stairs until he stood at the door to the master bedroom. His heart pounded. He tried to make himself turn away from the closed door, to go back down the stairs, to leave the house.

Powerless to stop himself, he reached out and pushed the door open. As it swung back on its hinges, the room was revealed, not as the cheerful sunshine yellow space Bonnie had made it, but as a dark chamber dominated by an ornate four-poster bed, its curtains drawn back to reveal a heavy brocade coverlet.

Then he saw the figure of the man.

He recognized it instantly, for its face was bathed in silvery light pouring in from the window.

Ed Becker was staring at himself.

And he was hanging, broken-necked, from the chandelier. The hands of the lifeless corpse reached out as if to grasp the living man and draw him too into the cold grip of death.

A scream of horror rose from Ed Becker's lungs, boiling out of him, echoing through the room, shattering the night.

Chapter 9

*F*or a second Ed Becker didn't know where he was. His mind still half entangled in the nightmare, he tried to twist away from the clawlike grasp of the dream. The terrible vision remained before him; he could still hear his own howling scream. Beside him, though, Bonnie slept quietly. As he sat up, willing his heartbeat to slow, his thoughts to focus, she sighed and snuggled deeper into the quilt, but did not wake.

Imagination. These hideous images were merely the product of mental stress—the culmination of months of anxiety over the awful tragedies among his friends, his worries over the fate of the Blackstone Center, capped by the close call they'd had tonight.

Imagination—overwrought and out of control.

Ed got out of bed and went to the window, where he could just make out the silhouette of his house against the starlit darkness of the sky. "It really was just a dream," he said quietly, repeating his wife's comforting words to himself like a mantra. *A dream. Just a dream.*

But he knew he didn't believe it.

Knew he had to see for himself.

Even as he opened the front door, he could sense that something had changed.

Everything about the house was different.

The way it smelled.

The way it felt.

He reached for the light switch, remembering the power had been turned off only when there was no response to his touch. Making his way through the foyer, he came to the dining room door. Though it was almost pitch-black, he could see the vague outline of a table and chairs.

Big, heavy furniture, unlike the teak set he and Bonnie had brought with them from Boston.

An illusion!

It had to be an illusion, born of the darkness and the memory of the dream. But then, as he remembered the vision of his clients' severed heads displayed on the table, he backed away from the dining room. Crossing the threshold into the living room, he stopped.

The room was not empty.

He could feel the presence of someone—or some*thing*— waiting in the space that yawned before him. As in the dream, he tried to turn away and leave the house.

But also as in the dream, his body refused to respond to the desires of his mind, and he found himself drawn inexorably into the room and the blackness beyond.

And then he knew.

They were everywhere. They sat in every Victorian chair, perched on every footstool, and leaned against every gateleg table and curio cabinet.

Two of them flanked the fireplace.

He could see at once that they were all dead. Pale, motionless, they somehow managed to stare at him accusingly with their sightless eyes.

Then, the wail. A low keening that slowly built into a cacophony of pain and suffering.

Ed recognized them all, for during the last fifteen years, he had studied photographs of every one of them. They were the victims of his clients, now gathered in his home, come at last to settle their accounts with the man who had defended their killers.

His heart pounding, Ed turned away and lurched toward the front door, only to find himself staring into the empty eyes of his long-dead great-uncle Paul Becker.

"They come for us," he heard his great-uncle say, though his colorless lips stayed utterly still. "The people we kill. They come for us every night. Now they've come for you too."

A moan escaping his lips, Ed turned and shambled up the stairs. His heart was beating so wildly he felt as if his chest might explode. At the top of the stairs he stopped, his eyes darting around the hall, searching for someplace to hide.

As the sky outside continued to brighten, and the silvery dawn began to seep through the stairwell's windows, one by one the doors to each of the bedrooms opened.

In silent ranks the victims appeared and came slowly toward him, reaching out to him just as his own specter had reached out to him in the dream.

Instinctively taking a step back, Ed lost his footing. For a moment he teetered on the top step, but then fell backward, a single panicked scream bursting from his throat before his head struck the bare hardwood treads, cutting off his shout.

Rolling over and over, Ed Becker tumbled to the foot of the stairs, to sprawl in a broken heap on the floor of the foyer.

Bonnie Becker raced across the lawn and up onto the porch of their house, throwing the door open so hard that the glass panel in its center cracked. For a split second she saw nothing in the faint light, then caught sight of her husband's body lying at the foot of the stairs. "Ed!" she screamed. "Oh my God! Ed!" Dropping to her knees, she was about to gather him into her arms when she saw the strange angle at which his head lay, and knew his neck was broken.

Don't touch him! she told herself. Don't touch him. Just call for help.

Her entire body shaking, she managed to get to her feet and stumble to the phone.

Picking up the receiver, she jabbed at the keypad, her hand trembling so badly she couldn't even be certain she had punched the right buttons. But on the second ring the 911 operator answered. Moments later, as she heard the sound of sirens screaming toward her house for the second time that night, Bonnie gazed numbly around the room.

It was exactly as they had left it.

Nothing had changed; nothing was different.

Yet as Bonnie went back into the foyer to watch over her husband until the ambulance came, she knew that despite her own words to the contrary, somehow—in some way she was certain she would never understand—another of Ed's nightmares had come true.

Chapter 10

*T*he first copy of next week's *Blackstone Chronicle* lay on Oliver Metcalf's desk. Though Lois Martin had put it in front of him nearly an hour earlier, he had not yet touched it. Instead, he'd simply stared at the headline—a headline he himself had written—and wondered if he could, in good conscience, let the paper be distributed the way it stood, or whether he should try to recover every copy that had been printed, destroy them, and start all over again. He was no closer to an answer now than he had been an hour ago. Yet the headline—together with its accompanying story—would not release its grip on him.

Local Attorney Injured in Fall

In the latest in a series of apparently coincidental tragedies, Blackstone attorney Edward Becker was seriously injured in a fall at his home early Sunday morning. The house on Amherst Street had been the site of a gas explosion several hours earlier, in which no one was hurt, and Becker, 40, his wife, Bonnie, 38, and their 5-year-old daughter, Amy, had evacuated the house.

According to Mrs. Becker, the lawyer returned to the house despite the possibility that it wasn't safe, and apparently stumbled at the top of the stairs. Fire Chief Larry Schulze states that both the gas and electricity to the house had been cut off for safety reasons. "I don't have any idea why Ed went back before dawn," Schulze said in an interview with this newspaper.

Suffering breaks in three vertebrae, Becker . . .

The rest of the story disappeared under the fold of the paper, but it didn't really matter: every word of it was etched in Oliver's mind.

Every not-quite-true word.

He'd spent two hours talking to Bonnie Becker at the hospital the morning after Ed had fallen, listening to her strange story of Ed's growing conviction that his dreams were somehow coming true, and how she'd awakened sometime before dawn to find him gone and had rushed across the street to discover the accident.

She'd also talked of a stereoscope that they found in the dresser Ed had taken out of the Asylum Friday morning.

Bonnie, exhausted and red-eyed, had looked at Oliver bleakly. "I know it's crazy, but I keep remembering the gifts people are talking about. . . ." Her voice trailed off, and then she shook her head. "Forget I said that, Oliver. What happened to Ed was an accident. It didn't have anything to do with the dresser, or the stereoscope, or anything else."

But Oliver had known even as she spoke that Bonnie didn't quite believe her own words. Nor did he. Yet when he sat down to write the story, he decided to "forget" the ruminations, as Bonnie had requested. No sense setting more tongues to wagging than already were.

And there was, of course, no proof.

No proof that the tragedies that had befallen the McGuires and the Hartwicks, Martha Ward and Germaine Wagner, and now Ed Becker were connected in any way. There wasn't—couldn't be—any connection between Rebecca's disappearance and Ed Becker's near-fatal accident. Yet Oliver couldn't help wondering. Still, despite his own doubts, despite the disturbing way his heart seemed to lurch in his chest every time he thought about Rebecca, it would be irresponsible to fan the fires of speculation. No point making people more frightened than they already were.

But Oliver Metcalf was frightened. Frightened nearly to death.

As the deepest shadows of night crept through the empty rooms of the cold stone building, the dark figure slipped one more time into the hidden chamber in which his treasures were stored. He didn't linger tonight, for already the hour was late and there was much to do. Lifting a shallow, oblong box from the topmost shelf, he wiped it clean of the thick layer of dust that had settled over it, then released its latches and carefully opened it.

With latex-covered fingers, he removed a tortoiseshell object from the box's velvet-lined interior and held it lovingly up to the few rays of moonlight that filtered through the window.

Its blade glittered brightly. So brightly, it almost seemed new. In the dimness of the light, he could only barely see the blood with which it was stained.

To be continued . . .

The serial thriller concludes next month . . .

JOHN SAUL'S
THE BLACKSTONE
CHRONICLES:
Part 6
Asylum

Unexplained death. Horrifying accidents. Murderous rages. The baffling disappearance of a sweet young innocent. No one in Blackstone has escaped the evil force that has spread through the town. Each strange gift has brought doom. Then editor Oliver Metcalf makes a chilling connection between the Asylum's hidden history and the terrible events befalling Blackstone. Is something unearthly doing its demon's work in this small town? Is it a sinister curse—or something far closer to home? And can evil be put to rest before another innocent victim meets a hideous fate?

In the final terrifying installment of *The Blackstone Chronicles*, no one is safe as the dark secrets of the past are finally revealed. . . .

Don't miss the dramatic conclusion!

THE PRESENCE
By John Saul

You can run but you can't hide. You can lock your doors but you're not safe. You can scream but you can't escape from John Saul's newest chilling tale of supernatural and psychological suspense. No one can outrun the evil of The Presence. Its dark, vaporous soul will permeate every corner of your imagination until there's no more breath to scream. . . .

BEWARE
THE PRESENCE!

Coming this summer
A Fawcett Columbine Hardcover Book

JOIN THE CLUB!

Readers of John Saul now can join the John Saul Fan Club by writing to the address below. Members receive an autographed photo of John, newsletters, and advance information about forthcoming publications. Please send your name and address to:

The John Saul Fan Club
P.O. Box 17035
Seattle, Washington 98107

Be sure to visit John Saul at his Web site!
www.johnsaul.com

Visit the town of Blackstone on the Web!
www.randomhouse.com/blackstone
Preview next month's book, talk with other readers, and test your wits against our quizzes to win Blackstone prizes!

TRUE TERROR

ONLY FROM

Schatten niles nmth

JOHN SAUL

Call toll free 1-800-793-BOOK (2665) to order by phone and use your major credit card. Or use this coupon to order by mail.

__BLACK LIGHTNING	449-22504-6	$6.99
__THE HOMING	449-22379-5	$6.99
__GUARDIAN	449-22304-3	$6.99

Name_____

Address_____

City_____State_____Zip _____

Please send me the FAWCETT BOOKS I have checked above.

I am enclosing	$_____
plus	
Postage & handling*	$_____
Sales tax (where applicable)	$_____
Total amount enclosed	$_____

*Add $4 for the first book and $1 for each additional book.

Send check or money order (no cash or CODs) to:
Fawcett Mail Sales, 400 Hahn Road, Westminster, MD 21157.

Prices and numbers subject to change without notice.
Valid in the U.S. only.
All orders subject to availability.   SAUL